GHOST LIGHT

a Nathan Active mystery

previously in the Nathan Active mysteries

BY STAN JONES

Vol. 1: White Sky, Black Ice
Vol. 2: Shaman Pass
Vol. 3: Frozen Sun
Vol. 4: Village of the Ghost Bears
Vol. 5: Tundra Kill

BY STAN JONES AND PATRICIA WATTS

Vol. 6: The Big Empty

other works

BY STAN JONES WITH SHARON BUSHELL

The Spill: Personal Stories from the Exxon Valdez Disaster

BY PATRICIA WATTS

Watchdogs
The Frayer

GHOST LIGHT

Volume 7 in the Nathan Active Mysteries

Stan Jones and Patricia Watts

BOWHEAD PRESS

Published by
Bowhead Press
Box 240212
Anchorage AK 99524

Library of Congress Control Number:
2020914044

ISBN: 978-0-9799803-1-2

This book is dedicated to Tommy Leonhard, who suggested the idea at its heart.

A NOTE ON LANGUAGE

"Eskimo" is the best-known term for the Native Americans described in this book, but it is not their term. In their own language, they call themselves the Inupiat, meaning the People. "Eskimo," which was brought into Alaska by white men, is what certain Indian tribes in eastern Canada called their neighbors to the north. It most likely meant "eaters of raw flesh."

Nonetheless, "Eskimo" and "Inupiat" are used more or less interchangeably in Northwest Alaska today, at least when English is spoken, and that is the usage followed in this book.

But this usage may be changing. The authentic and indigenous "Inupiat" seems to be gradually superseding it, especially among younger and better-educated members of the culture.

The term "Inuit" is sometimes proposed as a replacement for "Eskimo" in collective reference to the many branches of the cultural tree historically known as the Eskimos. But some Alaskan Inupiat reject "Inuit" in application to themselves. They argue—somewhat accurately—that it is a Canadian term referring specifically to Canadian Eskimos and should not be applied to American Eskimos.

A NORTHWEST ALASKA GLOSSARY

A few words of Inupiaq, the language of the Inupiat, appear in *Ghost Light*. Their definitions and pronunciations are given below, along with some English slang common in Chukchi.

aaka – (AH-kuh) mother

aana (AH-nah) — old woman, grandmother

aarigaa (AH-dee-GAH) – is good

alipaa! (AH-la-PAH) — It's cold!

angatkuq (AHNG-ut-cook) — shaman

aqaa (uh-KAH) - it stinks

arii (ah-DEE) — exclamation of irritation, impatience, or pain

atiqluk (ah-TEAK-luck) — woman's hooded overshirt, often of flowered fabric, with a large pouch in front

Kay-Chuck — nickname for Chukchi's public radio station, KCHK.

bunnik – (BUN-uck) daughter

kikituq (KEY-key-tuck) -- shaman's power object, often in the form of a whale-headed dog

kinnuk *(KIN-ook)* — crazy

naluaqmiiyaaq (nuh-LOCK-me-ock) — almost white

naluaqmiu, naluaqmiut *(nuh-LOCK-me)* – white person, white people

qanichaq (KUN-ee-CHUCK) — Arctic entry

quyaanna (kwee-AHN-uh) – thank you

ulu (OO-loo) — traditional Inupiat woman's knife, shaped like a wedge of pie with the cutting edge on the rim

voice out — speak for

yoi (yoy) -- expression of admiration or envy, often sarcastic

GHOST LIGHT

CHAPTER ONE

·*August 15* ·

CHUKCHI

Lucy Brophy crashed into Nathan Active as he passed her office on the second floor of the Chukchi Public Safety building.

She pulled back and told him, "You've got visitors, been waiting twenty minutes." She checked her watch and stuffed a pair of long socks into a bulky purse slung over her shoulder.

His office manager and one-time girlfriend seemed a little jumpy. She had, he recalled, an appointment of undisclosed purpose this morning. She had said only that she would be gone for several hours.

He had thought of asking what was up, but decided against it. For one thing, it might be something he was better off not knowing as chief of the Chukchi Region Public Safety Department. For another, he'd probably find out anyway. Public safety was an echo chamber.

He nodded toward his office, which was next to hers. An elderly Inupiat couple was visible through the window in the door.

"What do they want?"

"Wouldn't talk to me. They said, 'We'll talk to that nice *naluaqmiiyaaq* cop.' *Arii*, so rude. I told them I wasn't sure when you were coming back, but they could wait if they wanted to." She tossed her head. "How's the baby?"

1

"Another ear infection. The clinic put him on amoxicillin and he's safe in the arms of his doting *aana* until I get off. And Grace will be back from Anchorage tonight."

Lucy cut her eyes at the visitors and dodged around him. "Good luck. See you after lunch." She disappeared down the hall toward the stairwell.

Active walked into his office. The elders sat on orange plastic chairs pulled up to his desk. The woman was perfectly still with a sweet, empty smile, and a vacant gaze fixed on the wall behind his desk. She had silver hair in a bun and a soft, round body. An LED flashlight hung around her neck on a shoelace. Her hands were hidden in the kangaroo pouch of a flowered green *atiqluk*.

Her escort was stout, with coke-bottle glasses and the walnut-brown, weather-polished skin of an old-time Inupiat hunter who'd spent his life in the sun and wind. He had a silver mustache and goatee, and wore an Inupiat Pride ball cap with finger marks on the bill. He rose as Active entered.

He looked familiar, but it took Active a few moments to pull up the connection. They had crossed paths at a fund-raiser for the Isignaq 400 sled dog race, that was it. The man had run dogs himself in a younger day if Active remembered correctly. His name was - -

"Oscar, right?" Active put out his hand. "Oscar Leokuk? Good to see you."

"Ah-hah, Oscar." They exchanged the customary Chukchi single-pump handshake, then Oscar lowered himself back into his chair and put his hand on the woman's arm. "And this my wife, Tommie."

She shifted the sweet smile and empty gaze to Active and he caught a whiff of potent body odor.

"She lost her brain few years ago," Oscar said. "Don't talk no more. I gotta do it for her."

Active nodded to the woman and sat down behind his desk. Dementia would explain the smell, he supposed. Perhaps she wouldn't bathe or let anyone else do it for her. Or perhaps it was incontinence. Or both.

He stretched out his right leg to ease the burning that had been his constant companion since a bullet had ripped into his thigh the previous fall.

"Nice to meet you, Mrs. Leokuk."

She gave no sign of hearing. The full, round face was smooth except for creases at the corners of her brown eyes and her smile.

Her silver bun was tidy, he noticed, and her clothes were unwrinkled and looked reasonably fresh. None of which seemed to go with hygiene problems and the smell now filling his office.

"It looks like you're taking pretty good care of her," he said to Oscar.

Tommie began rocking from the waist, forward and back, forward and back.

"Yeah, she get along okay at home," Oscar said. "She still do her beads, her sewing sometimes, try work her jigsaw puzzle of Jesus in the manger. Our granddaughter come over and cook for us so she don't burn herself."

Active tried to think how to work Oscar around to the reason for the visit but decided to hold off. The quickest way to get an Inupiat elder to the point was usually to wait him out.

"So she's in good hands."

"Most times." Oscar studied the floor with an embarrassed look. "Except she'll go out sometimes when we don't know, walk around all night, maybe bring back a souvenir."

"A souvenir? What kind of souvenir?"

"Something she find on the road, on the beach. A button, a bottle, one time false teeth." Oscar chuckled.

Active smiled, nodded, and waited.

"Never bother nobody," Oscar went on. "Never get in no trouble. But last night..." Oscar's voice trailed off and he looked at the floor again.

Finally, maybe, some progress. "Did somebody hurt her? Is that why you're here?" Active opened his notebook.

"Nothing like that, but she find some trouble, all right."

Had Tommie taken a "souvenir" valuable enough to qualify as theft from a vehicle or even someone's house? He pictured himself cuffing Tommie Leokuk, fingerprinting her, and locking her up in the Chukchi jail.

"I'm sure we can straighten it out," he said. "What kind of trouble did she find, exactly?"

"Maybe you'll figure out what kind."

Oscar looked at the floor, then Active, then the floor again.

"Just tell me what she found, okay?"

"She gonna show you." He pulled Tommie's clenched fist out of the pouch of her *atiqluk* and pushed it toward Active.

Oscar murmured a few words of Inupiaq in Tommie's ear, and the gnarled brown fingers slowly uncurled to reveal a piece of human jawbone.

Active recoiled, recovered, and studied it as he pulled on blue nitrile gloves from a desk drawer. Shreds of gum tissue clung to the jawbone and a single molar was still in place. The molar had a silver filling, and the jawbone stank. Like a rotten fish on a beach.

Active lifted the thing from Tommie's palm. She looked at him and said something that sounded like *"Kikituq?"* Then the empty eyes turned bright and she giggled like a little girl.

Active held the jawbone up, turned it, examined it from end to end, and dropped it into an evidence bag.

"Where did you - -" He stopped and turned to Oscar. "Where did she find this?"

Oscar shrugged. "No clue."

"And did she say '*kikituq?*'"

"Ah-hah," Oscar said. "What them *naluaqmiuts* call a monster, probably. Most times, a dog with a whale head, big sharp teeth tear you apart. Early days ago, them old *angatkuqs,* they keep a carving of it around their neck, send it out at night to kill their enemies. That *kikituq* give the *angatkuq* his power."

"That's it, Chief?" Danny Kavik stared at the jawbone laid out on a sheaf of paper towels on Active's desk blotter. "Nothing on where it came from? Or whose it was?"

"Nope, nada."

Active's deputy chief pointed at the molar with its filling. "At least we know it's human."

"Which is all we do know." Active returned the jawbone to its bag. "Which is why God made medical examiners. Maybe Georgeanne can identify it from dental records. She's worked miracles before."

"Or maybe DNA," Kavik said.

"There was one more thing. Tommie said '*kikituq?*' when she pulled it out of her *atiqluk*. That mean anything to you?"

"My Inupiaq's pretty rusty...some kind of mythical - -"

"It's a kind of whale-headed dog that the old *angatkuqs* would - -"

"Oh, yeah," Kavik said. "The *kikituq*. A shaman's power object."

"Really?"

Kavik looked embarrassed. "Well, that's what the anthropologists called it."

"Uh-huh."

"I have a friend who's doing their graduate thesis on the spiritual beliefs of Arctic indigenous people, and they shared some intel with me."

"'They?'" Active said.

"All right, 'she.' She shared it with me."

"Ah," Active said. "And what else might you and this friend be sharing?"

Kavik flipped him off in a friendly way. "Mind your own business, Boss. So Tommie's saying some monster went out and tore somebody up and she found the body and now she's bringing in the pieces?"

"It could mean almost anything, I guess," Active said. "Or nothing. Tommie's mind's a blank slate. Maybe she just likes the sound of the word."

"Why do they let her wander around like that anyway?"

"Apparently she sneaks out while they're asleep. Oscar said they tried strapping her to the bed and rigging the door so she couldn't get out, but she got so agitated, they thought she might hurt herself. So, they make do."

"Like everybody, I suppose."

Active nodded. "According to Oscar, she'll get out every few days and eventually wander back again. Or a cabbie will bring her home. Or Oscar will wake up, call his granddaughter, and they'll go look on his four-wheeler. And he says we've picked her up once or twice?"

"Oh, yeah, I think Alan Long did that once. And another patrol officer a couple of times."

"Well, see where they found her, ah? We can check out those locations."

"How about searching the area around her house. How far can an old lady walk?"

"Pretty far, it turns out. It seems she's a tough old gal, like a lot of the old-timers. So we might have to cover all four square miles of Chukchi, and a lot more than that if she got past the airport and was wandering around the fish camps down in Tent City. Or if she got across the Lagoon Bridge and took a stroll on the tundra back there, maybe dug around in the Bluff Cemetery."

"How'd she get back last night?"

"A cabbie from Louie's, according to Oscar. She's on her way - -" Active stopped at the sound of footsteps in the stairwell. "And here she is now, I'm guessing."

After a minute or two, Active realized that Lucy was still out and no one was outside his office to greet their witness. He opened his door to a stocky figure in jeans, a T-shirt, and a worn black leather jacket. She had a thick hawser of dark hair down her back and wraparound sunglasses in the vee of her zipper in front.

"Chief Active," he said. "Thanks for coming in."

"Girlie Kivalina," she responded in a voice like gravel in a gearbox.

He waved her to a seat and introduced Kavik, then settled behind his desk with his notebook out. "I understand you picked up Tommie Leokuk last night. Can you tell us when that was?"

"This morning little bit past two, maybe," the cabbie answered. "I drop a fare off at the Arctic Inn, then I head home along Third. That's when I see Tommie coming toward me there by Sundog Park. Is she okay? *Aqaa*, she sure stink."

"No, no, she's fine. It's just that Oscar's worried about her wandering around like that and so we're trying to figure out where she goes."

Girlie raised her eyebrows in the Inupiat signal of assent.

"Did you ever pick her up before?"

"Sure thing, three times last couple months maybe. I stop, she'll climb in, never say nothing, just hum to herself and rock back and forth. I take her to their house, wait till she go in, then I leave."

"So she was walking on Third? Did she come out of a building or a house maybe?"

"No, she's already on the street when I see her."

"How about the other times?"

Girlie stopped for a moment to reflect, then ticked the memories off on her fingers. "First time, maybe a block from her house. Then one time by the post office and that other time by the Catholic church. But she never stink like that before."

Active noted it all down. "Thanks for coming in. If you think of something else, you call me, okay?" He gave her a card and walked her to the door. "And thanks for looking out for Tommie."

Girlie grinned, exposing a gap two teeth wide in her bottom jaw. "We ladies gotta take care of each other, ah? Especially if it's an *aana*."

She left and Kavik pulled up a satellite map of Chukchi on his laptop. He cursored around for a second, then zoomed in on the area between Sundog Park and the Leokuk home on Caribou Way.

"There must be at least fifty structures between Oscar's place and where Girlie picked her up," Kavik said.

"Not to mention a block-long park and the Third Street Cemetery."

"So how do we find the body?"

"First thing, you take Alan Long and check that cemetery to make sure kids or dogs or something haven't opened up one of the graves. And the Bluff Cemetery, too, while you're at it."

"Got it," Kavik said."

"And let's tell Patrol to keep an eye out for Tommie. If they spot her, they're to follow her around unless they get a call." Active tapped the jawbone in its bag. "Meanwhile, we ship this thing off to Georgeanne. And then we wait."

CHAPTER TWO

·August 16 ·

CHUKCHI

Active looked over the heads of the sparse crowd in the Arctic Dragon and took an empty table near a window in the back. Grace had made it home from her Anchorage trip the previous night, but so late in the evening they had barely had time to see each other. Now they were meeting for lunch and a catch-up.

A spike-haired Korean waitress brought a high chair and two menus as he surfed the news on his phone and watched the door. Fifteen minutes passed, then Grace arrived with Charlie in a front pack. He waved her over.

"Hey, stranger." He gave her a kiss on the lips, longer and harder than he normally would in public.

"Well, I missed you, too," she said with a laugh. She dropped a black and yellow flyer on the table.

He hadn't thought she could look any more beautiful until Charlie came along. The quicksilver eyes and dark, gleaming hair like raven feathers had mesmerized him from the moment they had first met in Dutch Harbor several years earlier. Since Charlie's arrival, she would complain that her face was too fat or she was too thick around the middle. Baby weight, she called it.

Not for his money. When he saw her nursing Charlie, rocking and singing to him, stroking his cheek, he marveled at this new incarnation of her loveliness.

Maybe he didn't tell her that enough? Between baby care, his police work, and her running the Chukchi women's shelter, not to mention parenting Nita, their teenager, moments alone together were hard to come by. An ordinary lunch date had become something of an occasion.

"Hey, big boy." He kissed the top of Charlie's bristly head and lifted him out of the pack and into the high chair. The boy smiled, gurgled, and waved his arms, brown eyes sparkling over chubby cheeks. Grace stuffed a blanket behind him. He was five months old now and almost able to sit up by himself.

"What's this?" Active picked up the flyer and read the title. "The First Annual Kay-Chuck Beach Cleanup Day?"

"The girls at work want to put together a team. I haven't decided. Packing Charlie while I pick up trash, I dunno."

"Maybe Nita and her friends?"

She picked up the flyer and studied the cover. "Maybe. I'll suggest it. Right now, I'm starved. Did you order for me?" she asked.

"Oh, yeah, the fried rice and egg roll combo. Do I know my sweetie or what?"

"You do, indeed." Grace unzipped her backpack and took out a jar, a tiny spoon, a bib, and a pack of wipes. "And how's the leg?"

"Mm."

Grace waited for more, but he couldn't think of anything.

"Okay." She uncapped the jar of baby food.

"And what's on the menu for Sir Charles today?" he offered with what he knew was hollow cheeriness.

"Rice cereal."

"Yum!" Active said, grateful that she'd accepted his offer to talk about something else, anything else, as long as it wasn't the leg.

Charlie drooled and banged on the tray of his high chair.

"I had to pry him away from Martha. That's why we're late."

Martha Active Johnson had gone full *aana* upon Charlie's arrival in March. Maybe it was because the boy was her first grandchild. But Active suspected it was also part of his mother's burning hunger for a do-over, her need to make up for what she'd failed to do for him.

She had been a fourteen-year-old wild child when she gave birth to Active and adopted him out to a pair of white school teachers, who promptly left Chukchi and raised him in Anchorage. By the time Active had been, over his vociferous objections, posted to Chukchi for his first assignment with the Alaska State Troopers, Martha had long since calmed down, married well, and produced another son. But it had taken Active years to forgive her for abandoning him, as he saw it, and to bow to the fierce mother love he now accepted as an elemental force of nature.

"Who wouldn't want to spend a whole day with this guy?" Active said. Charlie's face was covered with white goo. He blew bubbles with the rice paste Grace managed to push into his mouth.

Their order arrived and Grace dived on it like a starving wolverine.

Active dished the remainder of the fried rice onto his plate and claimed two of the egg rolls while there was still time. "How was the conference? Obviously the food was inadequate."

"Helpful," Grace said around a mouthful of fried rice as Active took a turn at coaxing more of the rice paste into Charlie's mouth. "We talked about identifying creative sources for funding now that social services have lost so much federal money."

"I thought it was supposed to be about education for abused women and their kids."

"Which takes money." Grace wolfed down the last of an egg roll and reached for another. "Like everything. And you? Find any bodies while I was gone?"

"Not exactly."

"Not exactly?"

"Only a jawbone."

"What! Whose jawbone?"

"We don't know yet. We're sending it to the ME in Anchorage."

"Where did you find it?"

"We didn't. It was more of a gift."

He laid out the story of the Leokuks' visit to Chukchi Public Safety the previous day and the malodorous surprise in the pouch of Tommie's *atiqluk*.

"Lucky you," Grace said. "But don't tell me any more." She'd finished off her second egg roll and now stared intently at the two on Active's plate. "Not while I'm eating."

Active sighed and transferred one of his egg rolls to her plate.

"Thanks, baby."

Charlie scrunched up his face and sputtered out the spoonful of cereal Active had just worked into his mouth. He started to squirm and whine, rubbed a rice-smeared hand into the black fuzz on his head. His face contorted, his mouth opened, his cheeks reddened, and he let out a piercing wail that turned heads in the dining room.

"He needs a change and a nap." Grace shot Active a look as she dabbed at the boy's gooey hands and face. He continued to howl.

"Sure, I'll take care of our little Superfund site while you finish your food." Active waited till she had most of the goo off, then pulled Charlie out of the high chair.

She looked at his plate again. "You gonna finish that?"

He looked longingly at the last egg roll and sighed again. "Yeah, all okay, go ahead."

A few minutes later, Active's cell buzzed from the tabletop as he worked a fresher but still fussy Charlie back into the pack on Grace's chest. He glanced at the caller ID, then Grace.

"Work," he mouthed as he tapped into the call.

"You better get over here, Chief," said the voice of Danny Kavik. "The Leokuks are back."

A few minutes later, he found the old couple seated in his office exactly as on the previous day. Tommie with her sweet smile and empty stare, Oscar with the look of a man whose late years were turning out to be more complicated than he'd hoped. Active offered coffee, which Oscar declined for both of them.

Kavik eased in and took a chair beside the Leokuks as Active dropped into the chair behind his desk. He waited to see if Oscar would start the conversation.

Oscar did not. He just cleared his throat and studied his hands.

Active decided it was up to him this time.

"Did Tommie remember something?" he asked.

"*Arii*, Chief," Oscar said. "You got another baggie?"

It was then that Active caught the corpse smell again. He

13

flinched, opened his desk drawer, and pulled out nitrile gloves and an evidence bag.

Oscar pulled Tommie's closed hand from her side, held it out toward Active, and gently pried the fingers open. A piece of bone with traces of flesh clinging to it dropped onto the desk blotter. It was maybe six inches long, and chewed off at one end.

"Kikituq?" Tommie smiled, rocked, and hummed.

Active and Kavik leaned in.

Kavik stared. "That's a - -"

"It looks like a rib." Active looked at Oscar. "Do you know where she found it?"

"Someplace she walk last night."

"And do you know where that was?"

Oscar squinted the Inupiat *no* and shook his head.

"Did Girlie Kivalina bring her home?"

"Not this time. She come back herself."

Active nudged the rib with his pen. "Could it be from an animal, a caribou or - -"

"Not no caribou," Oscar said. "I cut up lotta caribou, all right, and that rib ain't from no caribou."

"Not a moose, either," Kavik said. "Or a bear. Or--"

"Not no seal or walrus." Oscar pulled his gaze away from the rib and looked at Active. *"Inuk."*

"He means it's from - -" Kavik began.

"I know what *inuk* means," Active said. "This rib is from a human being."

"And still no idea where she got it?" Kavik said.

Oscar squinted the *no* again.

Active thanked the Leokuks, and Kavik showed them out as he bagged and tagged the rib.

"What now?" Kavik asked when he came back in.

"Off to Georgeanne it goes."

"To join its fellow body part."

"Unless they're from different bodies."

"How do we figure out where Tommie's finding these things?" Kavik asked. "Maybe put a phone on her and track her with the Location service?"

"Nah, what are the chances it wouldn't get lost or broken the first day she had it?"

"Good point," Kavik said. "Seems like I lose mine at least five times a week, and that's just in the house."

Active drummed his fingers on the blotter, studied the rib in its plastic bag, and turned it over in his mind. "I guess we have to follow her every time she leaves home."

"But how are we even gonna know? It's not like Oscar's gonna wake up and call us. And she doesn't do it every night."

"And we don't have the manpower to stake out the house all night."

"No way," Kavik said. "But if we could get an alert as soon as she steps - -"

A knock sounded on the door and Lucy poked her head in. "Nathan, could I have a minute?"

"Sure, come in."

"No, ah, privately? In my office?"

"We're kind of in the middle of - -"

"Just for a minute?"

Active looked at Kavik, rolled his eyes, and stood up. "Have a brainstorm while I'm gone, okay?"

Active followed Lucy into her office and shut the door. "What's up?"

"I want you to tell me if I did something stupid." She hiked her foot up onto her desk, pulled up one pant leg, rolled down the sock, and peeled back the bandage underneath.

Circling her ankle was a fresh tattoo, a graceful band of intertwined blue vines.

"Wait, you can get a tattoo in Chukchi now?"

She raised her eyebrows, *yes*. "My Uncle Oobie learned in jail." She looked at him with a plea in her eyes. "What do you think?"

"This was your appointment yesterday?"

She raised her eyebrows again.

"What made you want to do it?"

"It was Dan's idea. He thought it might be, you know, kind spice things up."

"On your ankle?"

"Well, the ankle wasn't exactly where he wanted it, but, I figured it's my body, so- -" She dropped her eyes with an embarrassed look. "*Arii*, you think it's stupid."

"Actually, I think it's beautiful."

Lucy studied the tattoo. "Really? Should I put it on Facebook?"

"I figured you already had."

He returned to his office, dropped back into his chair and grinned across the desk at Kavik.

"Everything okay with Lucy?" Kavik asked.

"Better than okay. She was actually a big help with this." He tapped the rib in its plastic bag.

"Lucy? She doesn't even know about the case."

Active told Kavik about the tattoo. "So, it's all about the body parts," he concluded. "We have a jawbone, we have a rib, Lucy has ankles, and Tommie has ankles."

Kavik turned up his palms in mystification. "And?"

"And we borrow one of those mini ankle monitors from

Pretrial Services," Active said. "And we put it on Tommie and - -"

"It alerts us when she leaves the house."

"Bingo."

"I'll make the call." Kavik pulled Active's desk phone toward him, then stopped. "But wait."

"What?"

"We gonna follow her every time she leaves the house? She usually comes home with nothing more exciting than a gum wrapper, according to Oscar."

"No," Active said. "If somebody makes a run for it, those things log their location every sixty seconds, and you can pull up a map of it on your computer. So all we have to do - -"

"Right," Kavik said. "We wait till she brings in another body part, then look at the map for that night and go everywhere she did."

"You got it." Active reflected for a moment. "But you know what?"

Kavik raised his eyebrows in inquiry.

"I think I will follow her the first couple times. I feel like I need to see for myself what she's doing out there."

Kavik's face took on a wary expression. "Will you be needing a, ah, partner for these expeditions?"

Active chuckled. "Relax, I can handle it by myself. It's been a while since I did a night patrol anyway."

CHAPTER THREE

·*August 17* ·

CHUKCHI

Active's cell phone chimed. Charlie squirmed against his shoulder and whimpered. It seemed only a moment since the baby had given up the battle with sleep and plastered himself like a limpet against Active's chest as he reclined on the couch. He grabbed the phone off the coffee table before it could undo forty-five minutes of rocking, cooing, and coaxing by Grace and himself.

"Shhh." Grace lifted her head off his thigh. "You'll wake the - -"

"Yeah," Active half-whispered into the phone. "I'm on the way."

"What?" Grace lifted Charlie off Active's chest. The baby flailed his arms and whimpered again. Grace nuzzled him into the curve of her neck and patted his back. He settled back into sleep.

"Tommie's on the prowl," Active whispered. "Her ankle monitor went off."

Grace yawned. "I'm going to put Charlie down. What time is it anyway?"

Active looked at his phone. "Eleven fifty-five."

She yawned again. "Have a lovely evening."

Ten minutes later, Active was crawling down Third Street in the blue-and-white Public Safety Tahoe, only the parking lights on, engine just above idle. Up ahead in the ghostly twilight of the Arctic summer, Tommie Leokuk drifted spirit-like along the shoulder.

The Tahoe's interior brightened in the headlights of a car coming up from behind. Active checked his mirror and recognized the ancient Crown Victoria of an old Bush pilot and dog musher named Mitt Zachares.

Mitt's huge white dog, by rumor half wolf and half husky, trotted beside the car. Mitt had gone through overflow ice far up the Katonak River with his team, and had lost three toes to frostbite. Now, he couldn't walk more than a few yards at a time and so was obliged to exercise the dog via Crown Victoria.

Or so the story went. Like most Chukchi stories, it was both unverified and unquestioned.

Active flipped on his lights, pulled over, and waved the Crown Vic to a stop. As he opened his door, the dog raced over, fixed him with its eerie blue-white eyes, bared its teeth, and growled low and steady from deep in its throat. Active slammed the door shut and wondered if this was how the *kikituq* legend got started.

"Maxie!" Mitt yelled. "Settle down!"

The monster backed off a few feet, dropped to the gravel, and cocked its huge head. The growling stopped, but the dog's eyes stayed on Active as he walked to Mitt's window. Mitt had long, unkempt, silver hair and a few days of stubble, but his gray eyes were as sharp as the dog's. He wore rust-colored Carhartt overalls with one shoulder strap unsnapped and a half-smoked cigar, ash-end up, stashed in a pocket on the bib.

"How you doing tonight, Mitt?"

Mitt opened his door and swung his legs out. "Can't complain, I guess. What would be the point?" He pulled the cigar out of its pocket and fired it up with the Crown Vic's lighter.

"Tell me about it," Active said. "Nice night for a stroll, though."

"Or a roll."

Active chuckled. "You do this often?"

"Yeah, but usually a little earlier in the evening." Mitt pointed up the street at Tommie, who was fading into the dusk. "Looks like I'm not the only one."

"That's Tommie Leokuk. You ever see her wandering around while you and Maxie are out for a roll?"

"Can't say I do. I know Oscar and Tommie from way back, but I haven't seen that much of Tommie since her mom passed on, let's see, what, about ten years ago? Then her father died a few days after that." He took a reflective puff on the cigar. "Seems like old people tend to do that, you know? Go together? Been on my mind since I lost Kathy last year. But I guess Maxie here still needs me. Maybe when he goes."

"I hope not."

Maxie rose off his haunches and edged closer. Active tensed up. Then the dog lowered its head and butted his thigh. He scratched it behind the ears and it groaned in what sounded like bliss.

"Tommie's folks, the Atoyuks, they were real old-time Eskimos, you know," Mitt went on. "Lived out in the country most of the time or camped down in Tent City till they moved into the senior center not long before they died."

"Tent City, huh? They have a tent down there or one of

21

those shacks or...?"

Mitt took a puff on the cigar and blew the smoke into the Crown Vic rather than out the window into Active's face.

"Can't say as I ever heard. Don't think I ever got down there to visit 'em."

Active kneaded his fingers into the thick fur between the dog's shoulders. "Well, you and Maxie, you enjoy your roll."

"You have a good evenin', Chief."

Active stepped back and Mitt pulled in his legs and eased away in the Crown Vic. Maxie took up his position by Mitt's window and trotted alongside.

Fire blazed up in Active's thigh as he climbed back into the Tahoe and started after Tommie. Physical therapy was rebuilding the muscles, but the doctor had said the nerves mangled by the rifle bullet might never heal completely. The pain could be with him the rest of his life.

And then there was the counseling. He had another telephone appointment in a few days with the Anchorage therapist hired by Public Safety to help him. He knew the drill after an officer shooting. You talked to a professional to make sure that you were dealing with it, that it didn't cloud your judgment on the job or ruin your family life. Last time, the therapist had asked him a lot of questions about moods and anger.

He accepted it, tried to play along and give it a chance. But he wasn't sure it helped, or that he even needed help. When he had started out as an Alaska State Trooper a few years earlier, there was a teacher at the academy in Sitka, a firearms instructor named Bachner, who'd been shot in the line of duty not once, but twice. One day, between rounds at the firing range, Active had asked him about PTSD.

"Cops don't get PTSD," Bachner had growled. "They give it."

Bachner was now retired to a big log house on a lake fifty miles north of Anchorage, complete with a Cessna floatplane at the dock and a life envied by every Trooper who'd ever worked with him. Sure, Bachner's old-school take on PTSD was way past politically incorrect in modern law enforcement, but Active was starting to see his point.

There had been a shootout. The other man was dead and Active was not. He had been wounded, but he was recovering. It was one of the risks you signed up for when you became a cop. Shouldn't everyone just let it go so he could move on like Bachner had?

He had Grace and Nita, of course, and now Charlie. He pictured himself teaching the kid to catch char from some icy creek in the Brooks Range one day, maybe as soon as next year. He'd put Charlie in a pack on his back, see how he reacted to that bolt of sunlight and silver as it came flashing out of the water.

True, he and Grace didn't talk as much lately. But he put that down to the demands of parenthood and the exhaustion that came with it, not the fire in his leg. The point was, he was fine, Grace was fine, Nita was fine. Everything was fine.

A lazy tendril of fog cat-footed across the road as he eased the Tahoe into motion and he lost Tommie for a few seconds. He squinted, tapped the gas pedal, and finally spotted her drifting down Third toward the airport. He followed her until she reached the fenced perimeter, reversed course, and started back up Third.

He thought maybe she was headed home now, but, no. When she reached Temple Avenue she didn't turn right toward Caribou Way and home. Instead, she turned left and drifted down Temple toward the Chukchi waterfront.

Half an hour later, he was parked on Beach Street. Tommie shuffled along the seawall overlooking Chukchi Bay for a few yards, then stopped, faced the water, and raised her arms. A gust of wind pulled the hood of her *atiqluk* back. In the ghost light she was a dark silhouette except for the gleam of her silver hair.

A four-wheeler sputtered past with a man at the controls and a small boy between his arms. The kid had his hands on the handlebars, next to his dad's hands, and a huge grin on his face. What could they be doing out at this hour? What could anybody be doing out at this hour? It was an enduring mystery of police work in Chukchi, one he had long since given up solving.

Past the south end of the seawall, a few skiffs and dories rode at anchor just off the beach. Farther out, fish nets with white floats rose and fell on the chop sweeping across the bay. It was the height of chum season and two of the nets had salmon flopping in the mesh. Some would go onto the open-air drying racks traditional in the village, some would go into smokers and freezers, and a couple hundred thousand would be air-lifted south to commercial processors in Kodiak.

A few yards up from where Tommie communed with the night, a man and woman sat on the seawall, legs dangling over the water, arms around waists. She kissed him, he kissed her back, harder and longer, she slipped a hand between his thighs. The man was slender, dressed in jeans and a windbreaker, long black hair spilling from under a knit cap. The woman was heavy and wore a red *atiqluk* with a design printed on it that would almost certainly be tiny blue flowers, since it was a Chukchi *atiqluk*.

Then the man spotted Active, pulled his arm away from the woman's waist, and spoke into her ear. She turned for a look at Active, too, and pulled her hand out of the man's lap. He realized he knew these people: Darla Koenig and Arthur Green.

Which was a problem. Arthur was under a domestic violence order to stay away from liquor, and from Darla, yet here they were.

Active considered violating Arthur, just to have something to show for this interminable night on the streets. But neither of them looked drunk, and Darla was clearly enjoying her time with the guy she had sworn in court was a menace to her safety. In fact, if Active knew Darla, she had probably initiated the date. At any rate, they both looked sober and everything was manifestly consensual. Nothing was going on that would justify the paperwork an arrest would generate.

Active turned his meanest cop glare on Arthur and shook his head. Arthur gave Darla a last quick kiss and hustled off down Beach Street, hands shoved in the pockets of his jeans. Darla shot Active the stinkeye, flipped him off, and started after Arthur. Active looked away, so as to officially not see if she caught up to him.

He shifted in the seat and stretched the always-sore leg over the console. A couple of minutes ticked past, then Tommie lowered her arms and started back the way she had come with the same floating, unhurried gait. When she was almost out of sight, Active wheeled the Tahoe around and resumed the slow-motion stakeout. Was she headed for the dismembered body? Or home, meaning the whole night was an exercise in futility?

His radio crackled to life and Dispatch reported that Monty Okpik and his father-in-law were at it again. The father-in-law had crawled in through a bedroom window and scared Monty and his wife half to death. Now, the wife was on the 9-1-1 line worrying that Monty would hurt the old man. Active told Dispatch to let patrol handle it and to call him if the situation got out of hand.

Tommie continued on through the gray twilight. She turned onto Caribou Way, almost certainly headed for home now. She veered into the middle of the road, stopped, and cocked her head right, then left, as if listening. Had she caught the crunch of his tires on the gravel?

She stooped and picked something up, something shiny. Active couldn't see what it was—a candy wrapper, a beer can, a fragment of foil from a take-out order? A body part? A piece of polished bone?

He eased up beside her and stepped out of the Tahoe. She looked up at him with her empty smile. Then she held out her palm to show him a crumpled blue e-cigarette, and said "*Kikituq?*"

"Let's get you home, Tommie." He coaxed her into the Tahoe and drove her to the house. She opened the door and went inside, leaving him with nothing for his night's work except the faint scent of sea air from the passenger side of the Tahoe.

"Refill?" Grace hovered the carafe over Active's cup on the kitchen table. Charlie rode her hip and sucked his fingers as Active marveled anew at the female capacity for multi-tasking.

"Definitely." He tweaked Charlie's pinky toe and squealed "Wee-wee-wee."

Charlie gurgled and bared his gums in toothless joy.

"At least somebody in this house got some sleep last night while his daddy was out chasing shadows."

"Nita, too," Grace said. "She's still asleep."

"Teen-agers do that, right? Sleep till noon?"

"I wasn't sleeping." Nita shuffled in, wearing a frown, gray sweatpants, and a baggy T-shirt. Her shoulder-length black hair was twisted into a knot and fixed to the crown of her head with a plastic clip. Claws clicked on linoleum as Lucky, her Jack Russell, followed her in. "I just need some me time in my room once in a while."

Grace and Active exchanged eye rolls over the girl's head as she slid her cell phone onto the table and pulled a bagel from the bag on the counter. She popped it into the toaster, sat down, and took Charlie on her lap.

"Such a big boy! Yeah, such a big boy!" She bounced him on her knee, producing more toothless glee, this time accompanied by giggles.

"You need a ride to the rec center, *bunnik*? I'm leaving in ten minutes. I'll get the dishes started for you." Grace gathered cups and saucers, set them in the sink, and turned on the water.

"No, I'll walk over." She handed Charlie back to Grace. The toaster popped. She retrieved the bagel and spread it with butter and honey.

Lucky yipped at the sound of "walk," scampered to the door, and panted.

"How's volleyball camp?" Active asked.

"Great," Nita said around a mouthful of bagel. She wrapped her arms around Active's neck from behind and pressed her cheek against his. "Morning, Dad."

"You, too, kiddo. Have a good day at camp."

Nita set her empty plate in the sink.

"You don't want another bagel?" Grace asked.

Nita shook her head and licked crumbs off her fingers.

Grace fastened the twist tie on the nearly empty bagel bag with one hand as she balanced Charlie on her hip. She glanced at a flyer clipped to the fridge door with a magnet.

"Nita, have you heard about Family Beach Cleanup Day? I was thinking of doing it with some of my coworkers. Or you and your friends could get together. Or maybe you and I - -"

"Ew! Pick trash up off the beach?" Nita looked up from a text she was tapping out on her phone.

"Sure. It could be a fun mother-daughter thing, right?"

"Uh, seriously, Mom? Do you know what disgusting stuff people leave on the beach?" She shuddered. "Like condoms?"

Nita's phone vibrated on the table and she snatched it up. "Hey, what's up?" she said as she walked away.

"Dishes?" Grace turned off the water in the sink.

Nita nodded and laughed into the phone. "Right after I take a shower," she told Grace as she walked out of the kitchen, still laughing into the phone.

Within a minute, the shower came on and Active noticed that Lucky had abandoned his post by the door and vanished, too.

"Me time, with a big emphasis on 'me.'" Active said. "That's normal, right?"

"Pretty sure," Grace said. "I kind of miss her though. The only time we seem to spend together lately is when I'm driving her somewhere and ninety-nine percent of that time

28

she's on her phone."

"How long does this stage last?"

"From what I hear, till she's somewhere between twenty-one and thirty. I was hoping for a mother-daughter talk on the way to volleyball, but …"

"You think something's wrong?"

"No, my mom radar's not going off here."

"Mom radar. Do dads have that?"

"Not that I'm aware of. Especially when it comes to girls."

"Well, I'm going to work. Where we have actual radar."

"Maybe you should use it to track Tommie Leokuk."

"Ha." He stood up, circled her in his arms, and kissed her. She tasted of coffee and honey. This was all the therapy he needed. He had no problem that could not be fixed by a session of skin on skin with Grace Palmer Active.

He moved his lips to her neck. Charlie batted at his jaw and fussed. Active drew back. "Hey, fella, what's up?"

"He's letting you know you're not the only man in my life anymore."

"Is that so?" He kissed her again. The baby whined louder and slapped at Active's jaw again.

"What, I need an appointment now?"

"Looks like."

"Well, pencil me in for tonight, then."

"No chasing old ladies and body parts?"

"Fingers crossed Tommie's monitor doesn't go off." He shook a finger at the baby. "I've got better things to do, no matter what you may think, young man."

Charlie stared and screwed up his face like he was about to spit. For a moment, he looked like a dandelion with black fuzz. Active couldn't help laughing. He headed for the front door.

"Hey, Mom!" Nita flew out of the bathroom in a towel, hair dripping onto bare shoulders. "Me and Gina and Mazie are going to win an Argo!"

Grace set Charlie in his high chair and swabbed his face with a wet cloth, then lifted him along with a pack filled with bottles, diapers, and extra clothes. "One of those giant ATVs? How are you going to do that?"

"It's first prize for picking up the most trash on Beach Cleanup Day. And we're absolutely going to win it."

"You're going to pick up disgusting stuff that people leave on the beach?"

"Mom, it's an Argo." She put her phone to her ear, restarted her conversation, and scampered back to her room, leaving a trail of wet footprints on the floor.

CHAPTER FOUR

· August 20 ·

CHUKCHI

Active stopped the Tahoe and watched from the Chukchi end of the Lagoon Bridge as Tommie ambled out and stopped in the middle.

Two days had passed since his last tour with her, and now her monitor had gone off again. Here he was at two o'clock in the morning, watching her lean on the railing of the bridge where he had been shot, the bridge he had been unable to cross ever since.

She gazed out over the water. A seagull wheeled up, hovered on the west wind, and examined her for a few seconds, then wheeled away and vanished.

She turned and headed for the east end of the bridge, where the road climbed up through a gully to run south past the Bluff Cemetery and, eventually, to curve around and loop back past Tent City and the airport and into Chukchi again.

He eased the Tahoe into Drive and hit the throttle. The Tahoe didn't move. It only strained and vibrated, and he realized that he had his left foot on the brake. And that it wouldn't come off. His foot would not let him drive onto that bridge.

The familiar sense of panic knotted his stomach and

squeezed his lungs. Before it could explode in his head, he shifted the Tahoe into Reverse and jockeyed the SUV around to point back into town. He waited a minute or two and his vital signs settled back to normal.

He checked his rear-view mirror. Tommie was still headed for the far side of the bridge. What now?

He decided he'd take the Loop Road in the opposite direction from Tommie and meet her somewhere on the far side of the lagoon. Maybe she'd even be in the Bluff Cemetery, digging out another body part from one of the graves, and this maddening case would turn out to be no case at all.

He eased the Tahoe on its way, then made one last check in the rear-view. And there was Tommie, now ambling his way. He stopped, shifted into Park, and watched her come up. When she was near, he opened the passenger door and she climbed in.

"*Alipaa,*" she said. Then she fell asleep, her chin on her chest.

After seeing Tommie into the care of her husband, Active turned southwest toward the airport. It couldn't hurt to cruise around a bit, let the bridge stress wear off, and see if anything jumped out at him. An unsecured door, some sign of disturbed soil or brush in a vacant lot, something that wouldn't look like anything until suddenly it did.

As he approached the airport, a light rain began to fall, misting his windshield and haloing the streetlights. The perimeter fence and the passenger terminal along the edge of the airport came into view and a hazy figure swam out of the murk about thirty yards off. It solidified into a man in a hoodie and a flat-brim cap riding a bicycle through the murk. The tip of a cigarette glowed under the brim of the cap.

All of which could only mean, Active knew, that the cigarette was not a cigarette, but a joint, and the cyclist was Kinnuk Landon.

Active yelped his siren. Landon stopped and straddled the bike, watching him from under the brim of the cap.

Active pulled up to the cyclist, shifted into Park, and stepped out of the Tahoe.

The crown of Landon's cap, he saw, was emblazoned with "LET 'EM!" That was Chukchi's unofficial motto, and Active had always thought it nailed perfectly the amused stoicism with which the Inupiat endured the shaggy disorder of the human condition.

"Hey, buddy," he said. "Good to see you."

"I guess," Landon said with a wary look. He reached back into his hood and pulled out a tiny tortoiseshell kitten. The kitten glanced at Active, curled into a ball at Landon's throat, yawned, and went back to sleep.

"This Buster." Landon stroked the cat. "He's gonna catch them voles and shrews outta my place, all right."

Landon had lived with his mother until her death two years earlier. Now he squatted on a vacant lot in a Conex shipping container. How any rodent could find its way into a Conex was a mystery, but Active didn't doubt that voles and shrews shrews did it. They would colonize any enclosed space that offered warmth or food.

As usual, Landon looked like his lifestyle. The clothes rumpled and muddy in spots, the long black hair stringy and greasy, eyes that always seemed to be saying a silent "*arii.*"

"Buster, huh?" Active rubbed a fingertip on the silken fur along the bridge of the cat's nose. "He looks like he might grow into the job."

Landon took a hit on his joint.

"So," Active said. "You got anything for me tonight?"

Landon blew marijuana smoke into the night air and scratched Buster behind the ears. "That Walter Charlie come back from Anchorage, all right."

"Huh. Dealing meth out of his mom's place again?"

Landon didn't speak, but raised his eyebrows, *yes.*

"*Aarigaa*, I'll see if we can make a buy."

"You could keep his Mom out of it?"

"She's not involved?"

"Nah, she never know nothing what he's doing. She's just old *aana* now, got that arthritis, don't hardly get around no more, even with her walker."

"Sure, we'll protect her," Active said. "Thanks, Kinnuk, you're a good man."

Landon took another hit and held it in for a long time. Buster started to snore, a tiny buzz against the sigh of the west wind and all of the other sounds that came from everywhere and nowhere in the dusk. Droplets of mist sparkled on the stringy hair spilling down his chest from under the flat-brim. "The sky is crying tonight," he said.

"Yeah, it is," Active said after a moment of silence. "Listen, you know an old *aana* named Tommie Leokuk, wanders around at night?"

"I guess I seen her couple times. Green *atigluk*, lost her brain?"

"Uh-huh. That's her." Active took Landon through the standard interrogatory, with the standard outcome: No, he hadn't seen Tommie coming out of any buildings, or digging holes in the tundra, or prowling a cemetery. By the time he was finished, Landon was shivering and stamping his feet as he sat astraddle the bike.

Active climbed back into the Tahoe. "You could get in,

buddy. It's nice and warm in here." Active turned up the fan on his heater to underscore the point. "You should get out of the weather."

Landon said, "*Arii,* I don't wanna talk about nothing." But he leaned his bike against the side of the Tahoe and climbed into the passenger seat. He took a hit on the joint, eyes straight ahead. The Tahoe filled with the scent of something like burning tundra mixed with rotten egg.

"You can't smoke in a police vehicle."

Landon started to pinch the tip of his joint.

"But I'll make an exception if you blow the smoke out the window."

Landon put the joint back in his mouth, took another hit, held it, and exhaled into the wet night air.

"How you been?"

"Same I guess."

"Still driving takeout for the Dragon?"

"Sometimes I guess."

Active knew that Landon delivered more than fried rice and cashew chicken, but he had long since directed Chukchi Public Safety not to take official cognizance. For one thing, anytime marijuana replaced liquor in a Chukchi house, Active counted it as a gain all around—for his town, for his department, and for the people in the house.

For another, marijuana sales were now legal in the state of Alaska, so Landon's only real crime was not having a business license.

At least it wasn't meth. Meth seemed to violate some personal code of Landon's own devising and thereby made him an invaluable source for the department.

"I can protect Walter's mom," Active said. "But I sure wish I could have protected that Annie girl, too."

"*Arii*, I told you already," Landon said. "I never see nothing when she shoot herself."

"That's because she didn't shoot herself and we both know it. It was that Roger guy."

"*Arii*."

"You know what will happen if you don't voice her out."

"*Arii*, don't say that again." Landon covered his ears and looked out the window. Buster fell onto his lap and woke up long enough to curl up and go back to sleep.

"I don't want to see you do it, but one of these days you will." Active punched up his voice to get past the hands over Landon's ears. "Because you know it's not right, that Roger guy walking around like he didn't do anything wrong and Annie dead like that. And what about her little boy? He's in foster care in Anchorage, did you know that? He's gonna be raised by *naluaqmiuts* and never know his own people, never know where he came from. What kind of life is that?"

Landon hawked, spat out the window, said nothing.

"A good man can't live with that," Active went on. "And you're a good man, Kinnuk. That weight on your heart, it'll make you take your own life sooner or later, I've seen it before. I just hate to see you heading that way. Your mom would, too, if she was still here. You know that."

"*Arii*, don't talk about my mom."

Active paused. Landon didn't speak again, but his cheeks were wet.

"So one day you need to tell me what you really saw at that party and take that weight off your heart. Maybe that day is today?"

"I told you, I never see nothing. We're all in the kitchen drinking beer, I hear the gun, I go in the bedroom, and there she is on the floor."

"I didn't believe you the first time you told me that, and I don't believe you now."

"All I know is, Roger tell me Annie get the gun and shoot herself before he could do anything."

"In the chest? Nobody shoots themselves in the chest. They do it in the mouth or the side of the head. I've seen it too many times. It's never the chest. You saw Roger shoot her and you need to tell me about it."

"*Arii*, leave me alone." Landon opened the passenger door and put a leg out.

"Listen, buddy." Active put a hand on Landon's shoulder. "How about you go talk to Nelda Qivits? She knows how to take the weight off of a person's heart. She did it for my whole family, and me, too, when I was having problems back in the day."

It was true. At various times, Nelda Qivits, Chukchi's traditional healer, had ministered to all of them with her miracle therapy of talk, sourdock tea, and patient silence. He was pretty sure that, if he could get Landon into Nelda's little cabin, her spell would work on him, too.

Active looked at the clock on the Tahoe's dash. It was coming up on three a.m.

"It's too late to go over there now, but I'll talk to her, I'll set it up, then I'll come find you and take you over there, okay?"

"*Arii*," Landon said. "I dunno."

Which Active took to mean 'yes,' because, always before, the answer had been, "No way, man. Roger's my friend, all right."

If Nelda could get him to talk, maybe a year-old cold case would crack open and a killer would go to prison. And a good man would be saved.

"Okay, buddy, I'll let you know," Active said.

Landon raised his eyebrows, climbed out, returned Buster to the hood, mounted his bike, and pedaled away.

Something was poking Active in the chest. He pushed it away and tried to remember what he was doing before the poke. Was he on the bridge? The poking came again, sharper, harder, so hard it hurt a little, and then Grace's voice.

"Baby, wake up. Wake up!"

He shook his head and opened his eyes and his gaze bounced around the bedroom in the gloom. A blue-gray midnight glow seeped in through the blinds. The clock on his nightstand said it was half past four. Their phones, tablets, and chargers on the dresser twinkled like a miniature city.

Grace switched on her nightstand lamp. "You were screaming again."

Charlie started to fuss in the next bedroom.

"'I'm hit, I'm hit'?"

"Mm." She raised her eyebrows in the Inupiat *yes* and waited for him to say something. He didn't.

"I just wish you could talk to me about it. You're scaring me to death."

"I know, but...I just can't."

"But why not? I mean - -"

"I don't know why not. Something just won't let me."

"Maybe you should see Nelda?"

"I'll handle it," he said.

Charlie began to howl. Grace shot Active an apologetic look, got up, and brought in the baby. She uncovered and hooked him up. He started making what Active regarded as the most contented sound a human could produce. He watched his bird-faced little son at Grace's breast for a minute or two, then leaned in and kissed her.

"I'm gonna watch TV for a while. I'll be back in later, okay?"

Grace nodded with a look that said nothing was okay. Then she locked eyes with Charlie and her face relaxed.

He slid from the bed, tiptoed out, and eased the door shut behind him, pushing back on the knots in his stomach and the iron bands around his lungs that meant another panic attack was on its way.

In the kitchen, he poured caffeine-free Diet Pepsi over ice, added two droppers of Orange Midnight CBD oil, and downed half the glass.

Then he swallowed two Ibuprofen and settled on the sofa. He dug the remote out from between the cushions, sucked from the glass through a straw, and found a *Golden Girls* rerun on the Roku.

He remembered watching the *Golden Girls* with his adoptive mother in Anchorage when he was a kid and finding it mysteriously soothing, even then. The pastel girls, as he thought of them, living in a pastel world, with thirty-minute problems.

Lucky trotted out of Nita's room, climbed onto the couch, locked eyes with him, and began licking his cheek with that urgent, anxious expression the dog had in all of their interactions lately. What, Active wondered for the millionth time, did dogs know, and how did they know it? He let it go on for a couple of minutes, then put the back of his hand to his cheek. Lucky went to work on his palm and Active returned his attention to the Golden Girls.

One of them was telling another outlandish story about her hometown in Minnesota, this one about a goat that could predict the stock market. The bridge and the dream started to slide away as he took another pull at the straw. Was it Lucky or the cannabidiol or the pastel girls or the living room with its picture window over the lagoon and the sofa that smelled slightly of the lavender scent Grace wore? Or the stubborn little stain in the fabric that wouldn't come completely out where Charlie had spit up strained applesauce? Or was it all of that?

Whatever, it was working again. The pain in his leg eased, the fight-or-flight cord stretched almost to the snapping point in his head started to relax, and soon he sensed Grace pulling a blanket over him and kissing his forehead as he drifted off.

CHAPTER FIVE

·August 22 ·

CHUKCHI

Active bent over the office printer and collected pages as the machine spewed out Georgeanne's report on Tommie Leokuk's souvenirs. He gave it a quick scan.

"Huh."

Kavik came in and dropped into a chair across the desk. "What you got there?"

"Georgeanne's report."

"And?"

"Not a lot here."

"Gender?"

"Undetermined."

"Race? Age?"

"Undetermined and undetermined," Active said.

"That can't be all."

"It is, but that's only what's on the record. If I know our Georgeanne, she'll give us the good stuff by phone even if she can't put it in writing yet."

He dialed her on the speaker phone and she picked up on the second ring. "Medical examiner."

"We want - -"

"Let me guess," Georgeanne said. "You got my report

and - -"

"And now we want the good stuff," Active said.

"This is not official, you understand."

"Absolutely."

"And you realize I only had a piece of a jaw bone and a partial lower rib to work with."

"Of course." Active opened his notebook.

"First, I would say that the similarity of scale of the parts probably means one body—but that's a pretty big 'probably.' The size of the bones, especially the jaw, suggest an adult female. They're not still developing like with a child, and male bones are generally bigger than female ones, particularly where they connect to a larger part, like the jaw to the skull. But a pelvic bone is the best indicator of gender. I don't suppose you've got one of those for me?"

"I wish," Active said. "What about the tooth? Any help there?"

"A tooth can help identify a body but only if there's something to match it up with, like dental records."

"There's no - -"

"National database like with fingerprints or DNA? Nope. A tooth by itself, you're outta luck."

"How about age?"

"The shape of the rib end points to a young or middle-aged individual," Georgeanne said. "Our ribs become ragged as we age, less flat on the ends. Twenty-five to forty would be a ball park, but, again it's pretty squishy."

"And race?"

"That's found in the distance between the eyes, the shape of the sockets, the opening for the nose, the shape of the brow. So, no skull, no race. Your old lady didn't find one of those either, I'm assuming?"

"No such luck. Can you tell how long she's been dead?"

"Judging by the recession of the tooth, the loss of surrounding teeth, two months, maybe three. Plus or minus."

"Anything else?"

"The DNA people are working their magic, but that takes a while. We did find some soil particles and we're having those analyzed. Might give a clue as to where the parts were found, indoors, outdoors, that kind of thing. Also, there are some tooth marks on both bones from scavengers and one end of that rib was chewed completely off."

"Dogs, you think? Or foxes maybe?"

"The teeth marks are pretty small teeth. Rats or mice, more likely. Whatever you got up there."

"We've got voles and shrews," Kavik said. "And ground squirrels."

"And there you are," Georgeanne said. "That's where the end of your rib went."

She paused.

Active rolled his eyes at Kavik. Georgeanne loved nothing better than a little strip tease when she had something big to reveal.

"However," she said.

"However?"

"Wait for it, Nathan. Wait for it."

"Pretty please with sugar on it?"

"Okay, okay." There was a grin in her voice. "Your rib shows another kind of mark that is pretty darned interesting, if I do say so myself."

"Georgeanne!"

"It's a nick from a sharp instrument. Most likely a knife."

Beside Active, Kavik breathed, "No shit."

"So it is a homicide," Active said.

"Another huge 'probably,' but yeah, it's unlikely this death was natural or accidental. I'm thinking somebody slipped a knife between her ribs and stabbed her in the heart. Somebody who knew what they were doing."

"Which would be anybody who ever cut up a caribou or moose," Active said.

"Or a seal or a walrus or a bear," Kavik said.

"Which would only be about ninety percent of everybody in Chukchi," Active said.

"You're welcome, guys," Georgeanne said.

They rang off, and Active studied his notes on what little they knew and theorized about the body Tommie was visiting. He looked at Kavik.

"We haven't opened any missing person cases in Chukchi in the last couple of months, right?"

"Not a one," Kavik said.

"Let's check with our public safety officers out in the villages, the borough cops on the North Slope, and the Troopers in Nome, see if they've had any reports, queries, rumors, anything, about a missing female in that time frame. Somebody's gotta be wondering why they haven't heard from her."

"I'm on it." Kavik started out the door. "I'll go down to Dispatch and canvass our village guys."

Active's phone rang again. Maybe something had slipped Georgeanne's mind?

No, it was Oscar Leokuk on the line.

"Uh-huh," Active said as Oscar spoke. Then, "Sure, come on over."

Kavik, who had paused in the doorway at the sound of the phone, raised his eyebrows in the white expression of inquiry. "Well?"

"Tommie picked up another souvenir last night."

An hour later, the Leokuks were seated across the desk from Active, just as on the their two previous visits. He smelled what Tommie had found even before she drew it from her *atiqluk*--a sickening sweet, musty smell like rotten meat overlaid with perfume.

It got a lot stronger when she dropped a shriveled, gray-brown finger onto his desk and said, *"Kikituq?"* with her vacant smile.

Kavik stared from his chair beside the Leokuks.

"Something bad happen to somebody," Oscar said from beside his wife. "Tommie never do nothing wrong. She's just an old *aana*, lost her brain."

"Don't worry, Oscar," Active said. "She's not in any trouble."

He pulled on a nitrile glove and rolled the finger over. It had been cut off at the knuckle, with little sign of damage to the exposed bones. The ligaments looked to have been severed with near-surgical precision.

He understood Oscar's alarm at Tommie's latest discovery. The fact that the finger still looked like part of a hand made it seem more human than the bare bones she had found before. It seemed to say, "Not long ago, I was alive. Like you."

Active deposited the finger in an evidence bag and dropped it out of sight in a desk drawer. Oscar seemed to relax.

"Do you know where she got it?"

Oscar squinted the Inupiat *no* and said, "Same like always, she wander off, come home, it's in her *atiqluk*. No clue."

"And did she get herself home this time, or did someone bring her?"

"Nope, no ride, come home all by herself again."

"Well, thank you for coming in." Active rose and extended his hand to the old man. "We'll let you know if we need anything else."

Oscar nodded. "We come back if she find any more."

Active ushered them out, slid behind his desk again, and retrieved the finger from its drawer.

"Maybe Georgeanne can get a print," Kavik said.

"Hopefully. In the meantime, let's see if we can figure out where Tommie found it."

Active logged onto the pretrial services website and pulled up the satellite map for Tommie's ankle monitor. Kavik came around the desk to watch over his shoulder.

In a few moments, they were looking at the trail of red drop-pins showing Tommie's journey through the streets of Chukchi the night before.

Active traced the route with the tip of a pen. "She starts at home on Caribou Way, turns right on Temple, then south along Third."

"Standard route so far," Kavik said.

"But look at this—instead of turning back at the airport like when I followed her, she skirts the perimeter and keeps moving south. Here she is down on the beach at the west end of the runway, now by the weather station, and next thing you know, she's way down in Tent City."

Active zoomed in on a cluster of drop-pins near the south end of the summer camping area and started counting.

"Bingo!" he said. "There's nineteen pins here. And no place else has more than a couple."

"And the monitor reports its location once a minute, so she spent nineteen minutes on that spot," Kavik said.

Active clicked to hide the pins and studied the terrain

where Tommie had spent the nineteen minutes. The blurry satellite photograph showed only an ill-defined rectangle ten to fifteen feet on a side.

"Whattaya think? A tent platform?"

"Maybe," Kavik said. "Or one of those shacks people used to build down there?"

"Mitt Zachares told me her folks used to have a site in Tent City. Maybe Tommie's been going home."

"We roll?" Kavik asked.

Active stayed in place, eyes on the screen. "Let's not get ahead of ourselves." He clicked the drop-pins back on and stared at the cluster around and in the mysterious rectangle. "If that is a house - -"

"And we go in without a warrant, then whatever we find --" He stopped at the sight of Active's raised hand.

"Might be inadmissible in court. Time to poke the bear." Active punched Theresa Procopio's button on his desk phone.

"What now?" she growled.

"Good morning, Madam Prosecutor!" Active looked out his office window at the gray drizzle and the state and national flags standing at full horizontal salute in the west wind that rolled in from Chukchi Bay. "It's another beautiful day in paradise!"

"Not till I've had a lot more coffee. What do you want?"

"To make your life more interesting and your work more rewarding, of course."

"Yeah, right. Just give it to me."

"I need a search warrant for an area within a fifty-foot radius of - -" He right-clicked one of the drop-pins in the rectangle and read off the latitude and longitude.

An extended period of silence ensued. Then, "What?"

He said it again.

"What is that?"

"It's the map coordinates of a spot in Tent City. No address, just the latitude and longitude is all we've got."

Procopio sighed. "All right, give 'em to me again."

He repeated the numbers. Her keyboard clattered in the background and she read the numbers back.

"And what is it I'm supposed to tell Judge Stein you're going to find inside this magic circle?"

"A decaying human corpse that was in all probability murdered."

Another silence.

"Seriously."

"Yep."

"So what exactly is on this spot?"

"Actually, um, we, um..."

"Nathan."

"Actually, we haven't been down there yet."

"Come on, I'll be laughed out of court. You want a warrant, you gotta have some basis for thinking there's a corpse on the spot."

"And indeed we do," Active said. "Just listen to this."

He described the process that had led from Oscar and Tommie's visits to his office with the jawbone and rib, to the rolling stakeouts on her midnight rambles, to the decision to put the monitor on her, to this morning's visit from Oscar and Tommie with the severed finger, and now the bouquet of drop-pins where Tommie had spent nineteen minutes the previous night.

There was another period of extended silence, then, "Well, I'll be damned," then more clatter from the prosecutor's keyboard.

"We should at least get credit for originality when I pitch this," Procopio said. "I never heard of anything like it before."

"Neither did we," Active said. "That's why we called you. If it was a normal case, we'd write the warrant up ourselves, same as usual."

"Cross your fingers. I'll hustle this over to the court myself and call you when I get a ruling."

"And we're heading for Tent City - -"

"Don't touch a goddamn thing unless it's outside in plain sight! Not if you want me to prosecute this case!"

Active cleared his throat. "As I was saying, we're heading for Tent City, where we will secure the perimeter with crime-scene tape and stand by. You've got my cell number, right?"

"Duh."

A few minutes later, Active pulled the Tahoe to the shoulder of Loop Road when the map app on his phone showed he was abreast of the spot where Tommie had spent the nineteen minutes.

The brush was thick here, and the Tahoe's windows were spattered with rain. No structure was visible. He showed his phone to Kavik and pointed into the murk.

"What do you think, thirty yards maybe?"

Kavik looked at the map, then at the tangle of willows and alders between the road and the beach. "One way to find out, I guess."

They climbed out, pulled up the hoods of their anoraks, and thrashed through the dripping, wind-whipped brush until, suddenly, they were in a small clearing a few yards back from the beach.

In the middle of the clearing, an ancient wooden shack with a tin stovepipe reared up like a shipwreck from a sea of brush and tundra grass. The walls were mostly intact, but a section of roof had caved in. A row of hollow-eyed caribou skulls with towering antlers stared down from an eave. A sheet of plywood was nailed over one window; another was open to the elements except for a piece of tattered screen flapping in the wind.

"Not a bad place to hide a body," Kavik said. He began circling the structure with his Nikon, clicking away.

"Just don't touch - -" Active's phone chimed and Procopio's ID came up on the screen.

He tapped the phone into speaker mode. "What did the judge say?"

"He said, and I quote, 'You had me at jawbone.' So you got your warrant, Nathan. Search away."

"Thanks, Prosecutor!"

He exchanged a thumbs-up with Kavik and they circled the structure to the doorway. It looked west, down an overgrown pathway to the beach. The door of the tiny *qanichaq* hung aslant on one hinge. Active pushed it open, and they found the main door into the house was missing.

They surveyed the interior in the half-light from the hole in the roof and the one window. A bare wooden table with a dented enamel coffeepot on it, an old woodstove shot full of holes, a forty-year old calendar open to April hanging on a wall, shelves still holding a few rusted cans of vegetables and chili con carne, and half an old Sears catalog.

Kavik picked up the catalog, flipped through a few pages, and dropped it on the table. Active pulled out his flashlight and began checking the floor. He found what he was looking for in the darkest corner of the room, under the good section of roof and away from the open window.

"Danny," he said.

Kavik came over and Active pointed his flashlight at the trap door with its rope handle.

"Looks like an old ice cellar," Active said.

"Yeah," Kavik said. "The legendary Eskimo deep-freeze."

Active swung the door up and leaned it against a wall. The cellar was just over waist deep, five weathered wood steps down from the house proper, and floored with loose boards on gravel, with frozen soil under that. Active took the steps, stopped at the bottom, squatted on his haunches and played his flashlight around the cellar. Kavik followed with his own flashlight and squatted beside him.

The cellar was empty except for a few rusty cans and other detritus on the floor, plus a couple of long-rotted gunny sacks hanging from nails on the log wall.

That, and a jumble of scrap lumber and driftwood in one corner with the corner of a black trash bag just protruding from underneath. Goosebumps prickled on Active's arms as he recognized the smell laced in with the dank scent of earth, water, and mold.

They hunch-walked over to the pile, heads down to keep from banging into the rotted floor joists overhead. Active tossed a couple of boards aside and jumped as something tiny and dark scurried across his foot and vanished into a crevice in the wall.

He told Kavik to start shooting with his camera and pulled driftwood and lumber aside until the trash bag was fully exposed. It had been chewed open down the middle by scavengers. He spread it open as Kavik clicked away, his flash strobing in the dark cellar like a fluorescent light with a bad tube.

Inside the bag lay a scattering of white bones and the remnants of a hand with most of the flesh chewed off.

"The critters have been busy," Active said.

"Like Georgeanne figured."

Active pitched aside the rest of the debris and they stared at three more trash bags in the flashlight beam. One was also tattered by scavengers, two were still zip-tied and intact. The smell built up in waves until they had to back off a few steps to gulp clean air through the trap-doorway. Kavik dry heaved a couple of times, then buried his nose in the crook of an elbow. "What the hell?"

Active took a deep breath and started on the bags. The one opened by scavengers contained an armless torso, mostly bones now, with maggots still at work on the remaining scraps of flesh. In the other two were severed arms, legs, and feet, discolored and swollen but apparently undisturbed.

"So where's the head?" Active walked his flashlight beam around the cellar. Then, from a corner, he caught the dull gleam of dirty, weathered bone. He bent lower for a closer look, then lifted a skull with the missing lower jaw and a few scraps of brown hair.

Active gazed into the hollow eye sockets as Kavik snapped photo after photo. "At last."

"But who is she?" Kavik said. "And how did she end up here?"

CHAPTER SIX

· August 25 ·

CHUKCHI

Lucy poked her head into Active's office. "Three more calls from Roger Kennelly at Kay-Chuck."

Active ran his hand over his buzz cut. "Tell him we're still not commenting?"

"I did. But I think he suspects it's more than just a random unidentified body."

"Thanks for running interference."

Lucy smiled and shut the door.

Active turned to Kavik, who was pouring a cup of coffee. "It's true. We're still flying blind here. No missing persons reports, I gather?"

"No females of any age over the last four months. From Nome to the North Slope, nothing."

"At least the way the body was dismembered isn't out yet."

"You think Oscar will keep quiet about it?" Kavik asked.

Active's desk phone warbled and he glanced at the caller ID. "All right! Maybe our luck's about to change." He scooped up the receiver.

"Georgeanne! Don't say we didn't give you enough to work with this time—three bags of body parts, what can you tell us?"

"Well, Nathan, you definitely have a young female victim, maybe five-four, judging from the leg bones, and the skull tells us she's probably at least part Native. Also, I found a couple nicks on another rib that show our young lady was likely killed by the thrust of a sharp blade like we thought. The markings on the rib indicate a non-serrated blade. Probably would have penetrated the heart and possibly the left lung. I'd estimate an eight-to-nine-inch blade. Sorry, she's too decomposed to tell us if there was a sexual assault."

"But nothing that says who she was?"

"Oh, please. You do know who you're talking to, right?" Georgeanne said. "That finger you sent down earlier? That little digit tells us a lot."

"Come on, Georgeanne, can you just - -" He caught himself. It was the strip tease again. You wanted to stay on Georgeanne's good side, you had to let her explain it in her own time. "Sorry to interrupt. Go ahead, please."

"That finger was the only one that survived intact. The rest were stripped by scavengers and maggots or carried off entirely. It's also notable for being the only digit severed from the corpse and for how it was removed. It was surgically separated, the same way the larger body parts were cut cleanly, the shoulders, hips, and upper spine."

"Why take the extra effort to cut off one finger?"

"Ah, well, the answer could be in which finger it was. The one that got the extra attention is the left ring finger."

"So the finger could have been cut off to get a ring - -"

"Which means the ring meant something to the killer," Georgeanne said.

"Now we're making progress!"

"It gets better. That finger had an intact print."

"Get out!"

"All I had to do was make a few incisions at the tip and lift off the skin to make myself a perfect little glove."

"Glove? You mean you - -"

"Yep," Georgeanne said, "I slid my finger inside it and fingerprinted our young lady."

"Well, that's above and beyond."

"I live to give, Nathan. You know that. Anyway, I ran the print through the FBI database and *voila*!"

Active could hear the pride in her voice even over the phone. "You got a match?"

"Lucky for us she worked at Prudhoe Bay for a company that requires background checks, North Slope Environmental Services, to be specific. That's a subsidiary of your Native regional corporation up there, right?"

"Yeah, they hire a lot of Chukchi folks."

"Not this time," Georgeanne said. "Your vic was from Nome, name of Shalene Harvey. She turned twenty-five on May eighteenth, probably right around the time she met her demise, judging by the body's state of deterioration and local temperatures."

Active looked at Kavik and spread his hands in question. "Shalene Harvey?"

Kavik shook his head.

"Nobody we know, apparently." Active asked for the spelling and scrawled it in his notebook. "Any theories about where she was killed?"

"Probably not where you found her, unless the killer was really meticulous about keeping her out of the dirt. More likely indoors, given the absence of dirt and plant debris on the corpse. But that's probably, not definitely. She didn't have any carpet fibers on her either and of course we don't have her clothes so...meh."

"But the murder scene, aren't we looking at blood everywhere? I mean, you kill an adult human, you're gonna get - -"

"Possibly not much blood at all, actually," Georgeanne said. "At least not immediately. You stop the heart, a dying body doesn't pump out a lot of blood. Our girl was stabbed on the left side and probably died instantly, so, if she went down on her right side, meaning with the wound on top, you might not find any blood at all, unless you can turn up her clothes."

"Huh. And what about when she got cut up?"

"It takes a few hours for the blood to congeal after death, plus or minus depending on temperature, so - -"

"If she was cut up within that period?"

"Then you could be talking a lot of blood. Not spraying out like if you cut into an artery on a living person, but definitely draining out while your butcher's at work."

"So - -"

"But I gotta say, I get the feeling this killer was a pretty cool hand, considering how expertly he dismembered her. So if he let the body cool down and then put a tarp or a sheet of Visqueen under her before he started - -"

"You mean we may have a crime scene with no blood evidence at all?"

"It's possible, yeah," she said. "I don't know as I'd call it highly likely, but a definite possibility, yeah."

"Well, shit."

"Stop whining. I got you a name and my preliminary report should be splashing down in your Inbox about now."

"Sorry, yes, of course, you're the greatest ME on planet Earth and the entire Chukchi Public Safety Department stands deeply in your debt once more. Thanks yet again."

"That's better."

Active hung up, found the contact for the Nome Police Department on his phone and tapped it. He spent five minutes on hold before the Nome chief came on the line.

"How's the weather down there?" Active asked after he and Gregory Kalamarides exchanged introductions.

"Clear as a bell. The Cohoes are in at Unalakleet and I'm headin' down there in my Super Cub as soon as we're done here. So, talk fast, Chief."

"I don't want to hold you up, but it seems that one of your citizens came to a bad end up here."

"Homicide?"

"Looks like. The corpse was dismembered, stuffed into trash bags, and hidden in a shack at an old fish camp. Probably about three months ago, right before breakup."

"You have an ID?"

"According to our superhero forensic expert in Anchorage, she's Shalene Harvey, twenty-five, most recently working at Deadhorse for North Slope Environmental Services. Last known address, Nome. Ever had any contact with her?"

"Oh, yeah, we know the Harveys. Not so much Shalene, but the family, definitely. We've been getting called out to their place at least a couple times a year for as long as I've been with the department, even when Shalene and her brother Donald were still teen-agers. Up until the dad left town about five years ago."

"DV?"

"Big time. Sometimes we were pulling Tony off of Janie, sometimes the other way around. Overall, I think Tony got the worst of it. He's a big, burly, white guy, and she's a little

Native woman, not more than five-two, but Janie is one mean lady."

"Did they beat on the kids?"

"Not so far as we could tell. It was Shalene who usually made the 9-1-1 call, and, more often than not, when the officers arrived, she would stick up for dad."

"When was the last time you saw her?"

"Shalene? Lessee, it's been a while. She waited tables at the Polaris, must have been not long after she finished high school. Pretty girl, had eyes somewhere between green and brown. Hazel, I guess they call it."

"Do you know who she hung out with while she was in Nome, maybe a boyfriend?"

"No, but my guess would be nobody. The whole family kind of kept to themselves. Donnie still lives in town with his mom. We've had a few run-ins with him for drunk and disorderly, resisting, nothing major. Shalene was the smart one. She got a job and moved out, it must have been around the time Tony took off."

"Can you think of any reason she'd end up dead and in pieces in Chukchi?"

"I got nothing for you there, sorry. Tony came up from Ohio, Illinois, someplace like that, and word is he went back there. Janie's a local, from King Island. I don't know of Shalene having any ties to Chukchi or why anyone would want to harm her except that she and Janie didn't get along so well."

"How do you mean?"

"I went on the call when they got into a shouting match in the parking lot at Shalene's job. Janie said something like she wished Shalene would have died at birth. What mother says that to her own daughter?"

"Yeah, the things families do to each other."

"Anyway," Kalamarides said, "I don't know of them ever coming to actual blows. Wonder how Janie will take the news of her daughter's death."

"I'm about to find out. I'm on the next plane to Nome."

Six hours later, Active was climbing the half dozen wood steps to the Harvey place. It was at the southeast end of Nome, a block in from the Bering Sea beach and next door to a rusty Quonset hut with a pickup on blocks out front and a sign that read "Big Don's Auto."

The house was small and green, set on blocks and skirted with unpainted plywood. The railing that ran across the little deck in front was also unpainted but the wood looked new. A big window was open a few inches, letting out the sounds of a TV and the dinnertime smell of frying fish.

Active did a civilian knock on the door—a polite rap-rap-rap with his knuckles—and waited a few seconds. Nothing. He escalated to his cop knock—seven hard, sharp hammer blows with the meaty side of his fist.

The TV went silent, the door cracked open a few inches. A thin, short Native woman peered out and scowled at the sight of his uniform.

"Janie Harvey?"

She half-nodded.

"I'm Chief Active, Chukchi Public Safety."

"Chukchi? Why you down here at Nome?"

"It's about your daughter."

She stepped aside to let him in. The living room was small, dimly lit, and sparsely furnished with a gray sofa, two wooden-armed chairs, an unpainted wooden cable spool for a coffee table, and an old-style picture-tube television. The only art on the wall was a print of a fair-haired, blue-eyed Jesus. The kitchen adjoined the living room, separated from it by a counter with chipped Formica. A grove of mismatched silverware sprouted from a rusty Hills Brothers can on the counter.

"Ma'am, can we sit?" Active asked. Janie stared blankly at him and stayed anchored beside the door. Active waited a few seconds, but there was no response.

"Mrs. Harvey, I'm afraid I have some bad news. We found your daughter Shalene's body in Chukchi earlier this week. It appears she may have been murdered, probably about three months ago."

Active had notified parents and spouses and children of the death of loved ones before. The reactions varied from hysteria to stunned shock, sometimes relief at finally knowing.

Not Janie Harvey. She plopped down on the sofa, lit a cigarette, took a drag, and clicked the TV back on, to a show about brides going ballistic. He might as well have said her pizza order would be ten minutes late.

"When did you last see her?" He had to shout over the noise of the television. Janie shrugged and kept her eyes glued to the ballistic brides. She turned up the volume.

He grabbed the remote from the sofa and hit the Power button. "Mrs. Harvey, it looks like your daughter was murdered."

Janie turned her face to him, took another drag, and squinted. "You said that, all right."

"I need to ask you some questions."

Janie waved him to a chair and slid the remote back onto

her lap.

"Have you seen her in the last few months?"

She stubbed her cigarette out on the lid of a Coke can and dropped the butt through the slot. "She take that security job on the Slope couple years ago, we never see her after that. Never see no money from her, neither."

"She didn't call? E-mail?"

"Nah, I never hear from her."

"Did that worry you at all?" Active pulled out his notebook.

"No. Just like Tony. That bastard, leave me with two kids to feed all by myself."

"Mrs. Harvey, I understand your kids have been grown for some time."

Janie cut her eyes at him, then back to the TV.

"Is Donald here?"

"Donnie!" Janie shouted toward the kitchen.

A chubby, barefoot, half-Inupiat of about twenty in jeans and a white T-shirt came to the kitchen doorway. One hand clutched a paper plate of greasy-looking French fries and a piece of fried fish. His cheek bulged with part of his dinner. He glanced in surprise at Active, then at his mother.

"What's up, Ma?"

"This cop says Shalene's dead. Seem like she got killed up at Chukchi."

The color drained from Donnie's face. He sank onto the couch next to his mother and Active smelled marijuana.

"Shay's dead? How?"

"That's what we're trying to figure out," Active said. "Were you in touch with her?"

"Now and then. She called me on my birthday."

"When was that?"

"My birthday? March ninth."

Active scribbled it down.

"Did you talk to her after that?"

"No. I tried calling her on her birthday in May but the call wouldn't go through."

"That was almost three months ago. Did you think anything might be wrong? Like maybe you guys should report her missing?"

Donnie looked surprised again. "She wasn't missing. Shay can - - she could take care of herself. She's the one always worried about me, you know? I figured she was just busy doing her thing."

"And what was her thing?"

"I don't know. She said she was making good money on the Slope, she had some new friends."

"Did she like to drink, party, do drugs, any of that?"

Donnie's forehead sheened with perspiration. "No, not Shay. I never even saw her have a beer."

"Do you know where she spent her time off?"

"She worked four weeks on, two off, and she didn't really want to come back to Nome when she wasn't at work. I don't know where she stayed when she came off the Slope. Maybe at Anchorage?"

"She ever mention going to Chukchi?"

"Oh, yeah." Donnie's eyes took on a sudden gleam, which Active figured meant he was happy to get a question he could answer. If Shalene had found any love in this family, it was from her brother. "I remember, she said she had friends there, all right."

Active scratched more notes on his pad. "Did she say who they were? Was she particularly close to any of them?"

"No, she never tell me."

Janie switched the TV back on with the sound muted and changed the channel to "Wheel of Fortune."

Donnie burst into tears. "Why would anybody kill Shay?" he cried. Janie scowled at him and turned back to her show.

"We're working on that," Active said. "In the meantime, if you think of anything else your sister said the last time you talked, give me a call." Active passed him a business card. "The smallest bit of information could be a big help."

Donnie wiped his face with the back of his hand and choked back another sob. Active stood.

"Just like Tony," Janie muttered to no one in particular. "Just disappear, never say nothing."

"Where is your husband, Mrs. Harvey?"

"Indiana, last I know."

"So you've heard from him?"

"Not me. The postmark on the birthday cards he sends to Shalene say Gary, Indiana. Every year since the son of a bitch left." She sniffed.

"Do you still have those cards?"

"I throw them all away."

Active glanced around the room. Not a single family picture adorned the walls, only the Aryan Jesus. "Do you have a recent photo of Shalene?"

Janie shook her head. "Why would I?"

He turned to Donnie. "Did your sister send you any selfies?"

The young man smiled. "Yeah." He looked at his phone. "But my phone's dead. Sorry."

"Can you tell me her number?" Active poised his pen over his note pad.

"Uh, three, eight, uh, I know it starts with three, eight. No, it was in my contacts. Sorry."

"Was her phone with the company here in Nome?"

"Seems like it," Donnie said. "I think."

Active shook his head and put away his pen and pad. The curse of the digital age. No need to remember anything, it's all in the phone. Until it dies.

Well, it didn't matter much. The girl's employer would have a photo and a phone number.

He walked to the door. "Thank you for your time, Donnie, Mrs. Harvey. I'm sorry for your loss."

"It's the eyes. They get you with those green-brown eyes," Janie said. "You look in those eyes, you marry them, raise their kids, then they run off. We fight sometimes, but why he have to leave?"

She turned back to the TV and ratcheted up the volume. Donnie hung his head and sobbed again. The fish and French fries slid off the paper plate and onto the floor.

CHAPTER SEVEN

·*August 26* ·

NOME

Active pressed his back against the plastic chair, stretched out his legs, massaged his aching thigh, and looked out the window of the Nome passenger terminal at the early morning light as he checked in with Grace.

Then he massaged his aching neck. Every hotel in Nome had been booked, and he had wound up spending the night on a bunk with no pillow in one of Chief Kalamarides's jail cells.

"That's right, sweetie," he said into his phone. "A whole extra day here, no seats till tonight."

"Oh, no," Grace said.

"Yeah. So I'll see you about eight-thirty."

"You need me to pick you up?"

"No, I'll get a cab or call Danny. Give Charlie and Nita a hug for me, ah?"

His last words were drowned out by the baby screaming in the background. He thought he heard her say "Gotta go" and he managed to get in a "Miss you, sweetie" before she disconnected.

An entire day to spin his wheels in Nome, when what he

needed was to get back to Chukchi and relax with a dose of Grace and the kids, with some reminder that the world still held at least a little love.

Maybe there was someplace within walking distance to get a decent cup of coffee. Then maybe some time with the Nome phone company to see if that's where Shalene had her account, then start working out the logistics of getting up to the Slope to talk to her employer. He stood and shouldered his bag.

"Hey, Nathan!" A familiar voice boomed across the room from behind him.

Active swung around. The owner of the voice wore aviator glasses, a leather bomber jacket, a Lienhofer Aviation ball cap cocked back on his head, and a big grin.

"Cowboy!" He stepped toward the pilot and his longtime friend with hand outstretched. "What are you doing here?"

"Workin', of course." Cowboy Decker pumped Active's hand. "How the hell are ya? It's been too damn long!"

"Since right after Charlie was born." Active flashed back to the time before that, last year, when he had been shot and Cowboy medevacked him out of Chukchi in weather that no one else would fly in. If not for the pilot's near-supernatural way with an airplane, he probably wouldn't have been around for the birth of his son.

"How ya been, buddy?" Decker boomed.

"Not bad. You?"

"Oh, you know, keeping busy, staying out of trouble. Mostly."

"Coming in or heading out?

"Out. Dropped off a passenger from Fairbanks with a load of mining gear and I roll in forty-five minutes on the second leg of my run. Are you working a case down here?"

"Yeah, and now I'm stuck here. The morning jet was all booked up so I can't get home till tonight. Too bad you don't have time for a cup of coffee. Be nice to catch up a little."

"Well, I've got some good news and I've got some bad news," Cowboy said. "I've got an extra seat if you want to leave now. But I'm not going to Chukchi. I'm taking a couple of safety inspectors up to Prudhoe."

"Seriously? I have to go up there on this case. I'll just make the trip sooner rather than later."

Cowboy clapped Active on the shoulder. "All right. Let me finish my paperwork."

"And let me give Grace and the office a heads up."

He stepped away to a quiet corner beside a Coke machine, checked in with Lucy, then called Grace at the women's shelter and broke the news that probably he'd be a day late, not a few hours.

"Oh," she said. "All right."

"Everything okay?" he asked.

"Other than missing you, yeah."

"Sorry, sweetie, it can't - -"

"- - be helped. I know."

"When this case is over, we'll have Cowboy drop us somewhere up on the Katonak and we'll kill some grayling, okay?"

"You kill them. Charlie and Nita and I will pick blueberries."

"Love you, sweetie."

"Love you, keep safe."

Cowboy came over as he rang off. "Time to saddle up," he said.

Active gazed out at the snaking rivers, tundra prairie and gray talus slopes of the Seward Peninsula as Cowboy climbed out of Nome and pointed the Lienhofer Navajo northeast for the two-hour trip to the epicenter of the North Slope oilfields. It was late August now, and the lowlands were starting to rust toward autumn. The ridge tops were still snow-free but, any day now, they would begin to dust with white.

"How're Grace and Nita and the little man?" Cowboy asked from the pilot seat.

"Everyone's good," Active said into his headset. "Chronic exhaustion since Charlie showed up, but at least he's healthy and happy. It won't be long before we'll be hiring you to haul us out into the country for some fishing and berry-picking."

"And how's the four-legged menace?"

"Lucky? He's in dog heaven as long as he's on Nita's heels."

"Great. I'll have to swing by sometime soon, have a visit. How about you? You doing okay with...you know, everything?"

How long would he have to keep answering that question? Active shifted in his seat and glanced at the two passengers behind them to make sure they didn't have headsets on.

"I'm fine," he said. "I'm done with the physical therapy. The leg's healed as best it can. Ninety percent functionality. I'm fine."

"How about your head?"

"My head?"

"How are you mentally?"

So even Cowboy was getting all touchy-feely now? "I'm good," Active said. "And thanks again for getting me out of Chukchi in that weather that day, by the way."

"No prob," Cowboy said. "It's what I do."

Active was silent, hoping they were done. Then he found himself talking again. "I do think about it now and then, of course, but I don't dwell on it. I mean, we can't change what's behind us. The best thing is to move on, right?"

"Not dwelling is not the same as dealing."

"Thanks, Oprah, but I have a real shrink. Department protocol."

"Well, that's good, unless you're just going through the motions. You know when I crashed at Isignaq a few years back?"

Did he know? The crash had killed Grace's aunt and triggered a long series of events that climaxed with Grace's being charged with murdering her father to keep him from doing to Nita what he had done to her. She had been cleared, but Active, in his deepest heart, still wasn't certain she wasn't guilty. He shook his head to clear it all away.

Cowboy was still talking.

"I had flashbacks for months," he was saying. "I started second guessing myself every time I climbed in a plane. I thought I might have to hang it up. But I powered through it and here I am."

They were over a cloud layer now, a sea of luminous white surf rolling off to a bright blue horizon.

"Powered through it?"

"Uh-huh."

"Do I recall that included three months when you didn't fly anything but a barstool in Nome?"

"All part of the healing process. Maybe you should try it."

"I don't think so. Can we give it a rest now?"

"Sure."

An awkward silence ensued. Cowboy finally cleared his throat. "So, what's this case you're working on have to do with Nome and the Slope?"

"We found the body of a young woman in Tent City a few days ago."

"Oh, yeah, I heard about that on the radio. Chukchi girl?"

"No, Nome. We got an ID yesterday. I talked to her family last night."

"Did they know anything?"

"Nope, and didn't seem to care much. She was working for North Slope Environmental Services when she turned up dead. I'm going up there to see if the company can fill in any of the blanks."

"Talk about a target-rich environment. Those people are tripping all over each other twenty-four/seven for weeks at a time. They eat, sleep, work, shit, shower, and shave within inches of each other. A lot of 'em are banging each other or at least trying to. It's hard to keep anything secret in that fishbowl."

"Like Chukchi, except more so."

"Yep. So how was she killed? Kay-Chuck didn't say."

"This is not for public consumption, but it appears she was stabbed, then dismembered."

"Ah, a crime of passion. It's always the same. If it's not money, it's love or sex."

"Which do you think, love or sex?"

"Same difference. Like I said, buddy, a target-rich environment. Target-rich."

Active closed his eyes and let the drone of the engines take him under. The next thing he felt was a jolt as Cowboy dropped the Navajo's landing gear and entered the traffic pattern for landing at the Deadhorse airport.

GHOST LIGHT

CHAPTER EIGHT

·*August 26* ·

DEADHORSE, PRUDHOE BAY

Active had visited the closest thing to a town in the Prudhoe Bay oilfields a few times before. What always impressed him was how ruthlessly industrial it all looked: a grid of roads built on gravel dikes to protect the permafrost beneath, with boxy steel buildings and hulking production facilities squatting on rectangular gravel pads. Here and there, wind-whipped flags of yellow flame danced above black smokestacks.

And north of the oilfields, the sprawling blue expanse of the Beaufort Sea heaved ice-free and lazy despite the looming Arctic autumn. The tundra here was already more umber than green.

The Navajo touched down on the gravel runway with a crunch, but no bounce, and rolled to a stop at the corrugated steel terminal. Active thanked Cowboy, who unloaded his other passengers and taxied toward a set of fuel pumps to top off his tanks for the trip back to Chukchi.

Behind the terminal, a dozen or so gray and white caribou grazed on the shores of a small tundra lake, the males already sporting antlers with the approach of the fall rut.

Which was another strange thing about the oilfields. The original inhabitants didn't seem to take much notice of their human and mechanical neighbors. Active had never been to the Slope without seeing at least a few caribou. And once he had seen a herd of several thousand crossing the Sagavanirktok River just east of Deadhorse and heading toward the Canadian border.

He hitched a ride in the rotting yellow Suburban that picked up his co-passengers, the safety inspectors. The driver took them along one of the wide gravel dikes in a cloud of grit and dust kicked up by a large truck a hundred yards ahead.

Deadhorse was the hub of the oilfields, the only place at Prudhoe where you could rent a hotel room or buy supplies off the shelf or catch a plane out. No oil was produced in Deadhorse, but it was where most of the companies working on the Slope had their offices and residential facilities. The oil wells themselves sprawled for miles to the east and west.

North Slope Environmental Services was in one of the Slope's standard metal boxes, a long, low one with a teal roof. Like all heated buildings on the Slope, it was set on steel pilings to prevent the permafrost beneath from thawing out and swallowing it up. A red placard on the door announced that alcohol and drugs were prohibited.

Next to the headquarters was a three-story modular complex that looked like a stack of mobile homes. It was also on pilings and was identified by a sign as the NES Man Camp. This, he assumed, would be employee housing for some of the rotating corps of Slopers who kept the oil flowing at Prudhoe.

A friendly young Inupiat woman at the front desk issued him a visitor badge and ushered him to the office of the operations manager. A sign on his desk identified him as Fred Sullivan. He was tall, ruddy, balding, and a little uneasy, Active thought, at the sight of a cop across the desk.

Active introduced himself and passed over a business card.

"Pleasure, Chief Active." Sullivan stood and put out his hand. "How can we help you?"

Behind Sullivan, the wall was spread with photos of employees getting awards or posing at job sites.

"I have some questions about one of your employees," Active said. "A woman - -"

A scrabbling noise came from behind the desk as Sullivan sat down. Frantic yips and yaps followed.

Active craned his neck and spotted the corner of a small kennel poking out from behind the desk. A small black nose pressed against the wire mesh in front.

"That your assistant there?"

Sullivan looked down at the kennel. "Yep, that's Chiquita. She goes wherever I go. I used to leave her in Anchorage when I came up here. But the wife doesn't care for her and I missed her." He put a finger through the mesh. Chiquita licked it. "Isn't that right, baby? Daddy missed his little Quita, didn't he?"

"A Chihuahua, right? Doesn't seem like much of an Alaska dog," Active said.

"Nah, she'll never make the Iditarod, but we understand each other." Sullivan pulled a stick of jerky from a drawer and pushed it through the mesh.

"That'll keep her busy for a while," he said. "You say you've got some questions about one of our employees?"

"Shalene Harvey."

Sullivan's eyebrows twitched. "Shalene? Great young gal,

good worker until she wasn't. Rotated out in May, never came back. Didn't call, didn't e-mail, nothing, just didn't show, ghosting I guess the kids call it these days. We waited a month, but finally we had to terminate her. She get herself in some kind of trouble?"

"So to speak. She's dead, Mr. Sullivan. Someone killed her and dumped her in an abandoned house in Chukchi."

Sullivan jerked back in his chair. "Dead? Jesus Christ. That's terrible. I never would have thought...I mean, what? How?"

Active retrieved his pen and notebook from his pocket. "That's what we're trying to figure out. How did she get along with her coworkers here?"

"Great security officer. Cooperative, always a pleasure to work with. The different departments don't have much contact with each other during their shifts, but we all get together every morning for a safety meeting. Everyone liked her."

"No issues with anybody?"

Sullivan rubbed his jaw. "Well, yeah, there was this one guy, Larry Hayden, a heavy equipment operator. She complained about him giving her a hard time when she first came on the job about a year and a half ago. She accused him of saying inappropriate sexual things to her. She came to my office crying a couple of times."

"What did you do?"

"I talked to Larry. He denied it. It was a he-said-she-said, so there was nothing we could do. Until that time he got into it with Josh McCarran, one of our mechanic apprentices. Larry had backed Shalene into a corner and he put his hands on her."

"Put his hands on her how?"

"Squeezed her boobs and went 'Honk-honk!' Josh saw what was going on and rushed in to help her. He laid Larry out. I had grounds to fire 'em both, but the other guys backed up Shalene and Josh."

"What happened to Larry?"

"He lost some pay and got a final warning in his file, which means his ass is mine if he does anything like that again. Josh just got a warning, which I thought even that was too much because I personally felt like he was totally justified in what he did. When Larry came back, we sent him to sexual-harassment training and changed his rotation so he was never on shift at the same time as Shalene and Josh."

"And this was when?"

"Hmm, April, I think. Let's see, Shalene made a written statement, I can get that for you." Sullivan picked up his phone and punched a button. "Molly, can you pull Shalene Harvey's file for me?"

A couple of minutes later a thirty-ish and moderately pregnant Inupiat woman came in and laid the file on Sullivan's desk. He leafed through it for a few seconds.

"Yeah, here we are, April seventeenth was the dustup between Larry and Josh. We sent Larry home early on April twenty-fifth. He wasn't due to leave until May fourteenth, the last day that Shalene worked, so he lost three weeks pay out of it."

"Do you have a photo of Shalene there?"

"Yes, here's her employee ID photo." Sullivan handed the picture to Active.

The image of a jawless skull discarded in the dirt faded from his mind as a young woman's face gazed back at him. Hazel eyes above a sunny, open smile that was a little crooked on the right, dazzling white teeth, waves of golden-brown hair falling over her shoulders. She looked closer to eighteen than twenty-five. He marveled, not for the first time, at how normal murder victims usually looked, how capable of happiness, in photos like this. So, for that matter, did their killers, often as not.

Active copied the picture onto his phone and handed it back to Sullivan. "Can I get a copy of that file? And the files for McCarran and Hayden."

"Of course."

"When was Shalene due back on shift?"

"Toward the end of May as I recall. That would be in her payroll records. I can call that up here..." He tapped on his keyboard. "Yeah. May twenty-eighth."

"You said you mailed her a termination notice. To what address?"

Sullivan flipped through the employee file again. "We sent it to Nome. Her home address, as far as we knew."

"Did her final paycheck go there, too?"

"Probably direct - -" He scanned the pages at the front of the file. "Yeah, she was on direct deposit with Wells Fargo."

"Any idea why she'd take her R&R in Chukchi?"

"She was visiting someone there, maybe? We have a few employees from that area, but I can't say how many exactly. You know, people come and go."

"I'll need a list of those employees, anyone who has a Chukchi address on record from January through the present."

"Not a problem." Sullivan tapped on his computer and Active heard the swish of an e-mail being sent.

"Is Hayden on the Slope now?"

"Yes. He came back up yesterday. He's due at work in a couple of hours. You should be able to find him at employee housing in our mancamp. Easy walk, it's right next door."

"Saw it on my way in," Active said.

"Right. Well, if you want to swing by here after, I'll have those files ready for you."

"Thanks, Mr. Sullivan, I think we're done for now."

Sullivan rubbed the back of his head with a one-more-thing look on his face.

"Anything to add?" Active asked.

"Well, it's just that, well, the guys up here are kinda rough around the edges. I mean, it's the oilfields, you know? A woman wants to work on the Slope, she can't really be a shrinking violet. I'd hate to blow that incident with Larry out of proportion and get him into any more trouble. He kind of paid the price already, you know what I mean?"

"Noted. But we are talking about murder here."

Larry Hayden turned out to be lanky and middle-aged and dressed in jeans and a smelly wife-beater undershirt. Just now, he was propping a raised arm on the door jamb and giving Active the eye. Gray-streaked brown hair stood up in spikes like he had just rolled out of bed and white stubble covered his jaw. He worked his tongue against the back of a discolored front tooth.

"What's this about?"

Active recoiled from the reek of the armpit pretty much in his face. "Shalene Harvey."

"That bitch? What'd she say about me now?"

"She's not saying anything. She's dead."

"Dead?" Hayden deflated some. "Fuck, what's that got to do with me?"

Hayden stepped back and Active eased into the room. It stank of body odor and stale microwave popcorn. Rumpled sheets hung off one of the two beds. A pile of clothing lay on the floor.

"I heard you don't take rejection well. If a young lady like Shalene says 'no,' you think that gives you the right to assault her. That jog your memory any?"

"Assault? That wasn't nothing but a misunderstanding."

"A misunderstanding that got you an ass whipping, cost you some pay, and put you one step away from being fired," Active said. "That could make a guy pretty mad."

"What the fuck, you think I killed her?"

"Were you at work the last half of May?"

A grin spread over Hayden's face. "I went to Fairbanks for knee surgery on May second, had it done earlier than expected, thanks to a change in schedule. I was recuperating at my sister's house for six weeks, and I wasn't cleared to fly for two more weeks. I didn't get back up here till June twenty-eighth."

"I'll follow up on your alibi. I need your sister's name and contact info." He handed Hayden a pen and a page from his notebook.

"You know whose alibi you should check? Josh McCarran."

"Why's that?"

"'Cause after he hit me with that lucky punch, he and Shalene got real lovey-dovey." Hayden passed back the pen and paper. "Used to sit together at the safety meetings, they'd get all kissy-face when they passed each other on the site if they thought nobody was looking."

"But you were?"

Hayden shrugged. "Anyway, when I got back up here

after my surgery, I ran into McCarran in the snack bar."

"I thought they switched your shift so you two wouldn't be on at the same time."

"Yeah, they did. But I guess he asked to change shifts after his May R&R, so then we were up here at the same time again. I wondered if it had anything to do with Shalene, so I said, I swear I couldn't help it, I said, 'Trouble in paradise, McCarran? Shalene get tired of your little boy dick and move on to something bigger and better?' He made like he was gonna take another swing at me, so I reminded him that both of our asses would be grass if he did. He stomped off, but he looked ready to explode."

"Is he up here now?"

"I haven't seen him. He bunks in another building."

Active tucked his notebook and pen back in his pocket. "Thank you for the information, Mr. Hayden."

He gave Hayden a business card and was halfway down the hall, when there was a yell from behind him.

"Hey, Chief! I watch those cop shows, you know. It's always the husband or the boyfriend, am I right?"

GHOST LIGHT

CHAPTER NINE

· August 26 ·

DEADHORSE, PRUDHOE BAY

Active picked up his file copies and the list of Chukchi employees from the North Slope Environmental Services offices, then walked the hundred yards to the maintenance shop where he'd been advised he would find Josh McCarran.

A big-bearded, big-bellied supervisor led Active to a man in greasy Carhartts, head buried under the hood of a yellow Chevy flatbed. "Hey, McCarran, cop here wants to talk to you."

McCarran pulled his head out of the flatbed's engine compartment. He had a muscular torso, square jaw, curly black hair, a thick beard, gray-green eyes, and a ready smile. Ruggedly handsome, Active supposed women would call him. It was easy to imagine him sweeping a village girl off her feet.

They moved to a break room away from the shop noise and took a table in the corner. Active introduced himself and told McCarran the purpose of the visit. His easy smile faded.

"Shay's dead? What the hell!" McCarran turned away and wiped his eyes with the corner of a red shop towel. "When? How?"

"When was the last time you saw her?" Active drew his notebook and pen from his shirt pocket.

"In May, when we both left for R&R. I remember it was around the middle of the month because we had just had the Cinco de Mayo party. She was perfectly fine."

"How long did you have off?"

"Four weeks on, two weeks off, just like her."

"Where did you go for your two off?"

"Home, to Anchorage."

"What about Shalene?"

"She was gonna stay with me in Anchorage this time."

"This time?"

"Shay had been staying in Chukchi on her time off. She had a, uh, a girlfriend there. Is that where she...where you found her?"

"You said she was going to stay in Anchorage. Why would she be in Chukchi?"

"We left the Slope together for Anchorage. But she wanted to go up to Chukchi to get her stuff from the girlfriend and make a clean break. I went with her. I wanted to be there if she needed me."

"Girlfriend as in - -"

"Yeah, exactly."

"So, you went along to make sure she didn't change her mind?"

"Well, sure. But she let that dyke wildlife hazer talk her into staying, otherwise maybe she would still be..." McCarran's voice trailed off and he wiped his eyes again.

"Wildlife hazer?"

"Yeah, you know. They keep caribou off the runway, polar bears away from the work crews, that kind of thing. They use rubber slugs, noise deterrent rounds."

"And Shalene was involved with this particular hazer?"

"Right. Kim. She was kind of controlling and Shay just went along. They had been together for a while. But Shay was no dyke. She was just confused is all. Like a lot of these village girls, they..."

"I know," Active said. "I went to her mom's place in Nome. Not a lot of love in that house. But it sounds like you had a real problem with this Kim ... what's her last name?"

"Tulimaq."

Active added it to his notes. "Maybe you were jealous?"

"A little bit, of course. But mostly I just knew Shay didn't need to be around that, to be taken advantage of like that."

"You must have been pretty close to her to know what she needed."

"We were getting there. We talked a lot, about her family, how she grew up in Nome, how she felt about things."

"So this R&R in Anchorage was more than just a one-time thing?"

McCarran twisted the grease rag in his hand, pocketed it, then took it out again. "We dated for a couple of months when she and Kim were kind of on the outs. Like I said, we were getting there."

"But you were into her more than she was you?"

"Not exactly. We were good if Kim wasn't around, really good. I thought maybe we could make it work if I could get Shay away from her for a couple of weeks."

"So what happened?"

"I'm not sure. All I know is, she decided to stay with Kim. I was waiting at the airport while she picked up her stuff at Kim's. We were going out on the same plane we came in on at twelve-forty, I think it was. She was taking longer than she should have, and then around noon, they announced the TSA computers were down, and our flight was gonna be delayed for at least four hours. So, I texted her to let her know about the delay and asked her what was taking her so long.

"Did she text back?"

"Yeah, 'OMW.'"

"On my way."

McCarran nodded.

"She was on her way," Active said. "So she meets you at the airport and breaks up with you for the wildlife hazer?"

"No, I mean, she never arrived at the airport. She texted back later that she was working it out with Kim, and she wanted me to stay away. She didn't want to see me."

"You never know with a woman, do you? Do you still have those texts?"

"I think so. Let me check." McCarran pulled his phone out of a pocket and scrolled with his thumb. "This'll take a minute."

"Some of your coworkers say you two were getting pretty thick, practically joined at the hip. And then she dumps you by text? That didn't piss you off?"

McCarran stopped scrolling and shifted his weight on the seat.

"Sure, I was upset, but I figured you can't make somebody feel what they don't feel. She was a sweet girl and a lot of fun, I thought we really clicked. I was even gonna take her to meet my family when we were in Anchorage. I wasn't pissed, I just knew when to stop pushing. My plan was to stay away from her like she asked."

"And that's why you asked to change your shift rotation after your May R&R."

"Yeah. I thought it would be kind of a problem to keep

running into her at work, you know? I didn't want to stress her out."

"You were looking out for her?"

McCarran rubbed the back of his neck. "Kinda. She took a lot of ribbing about her personal life. I didn't want to make it worse."

"Why do you think she got hassled?"

"Well, she was a young pretty girl working on the Slope, kind of quiet and...well, a village girl, not tough and hard like you have to be up here. Some of these guys, they feel like this is man country. Maybe they thought if they hassled her enough, she'd quit.

McCarran pulled at his beard.

"And lot of 'em wanted to get in her pants, of course, and they didn't like being told 'no.' And then, her being a lesbian, or at least with one, that didn't help."

"Anyone in particular bothering her?"

"This one old guy, Larry. I had to straighten him out once."

"You hit him?"

"Son of a bitch had it coming."

"You punch a guy out for hassling her but you don't fight to take her away from another woman?"

McCarran squared his jaw and set down his phone. "What're you trying to say? I could've made a big deal about it, but what good was that going to do? I figured if she could go back to Kim that easy, she was never all in with me in the first place."

"I guess you'll never know, right?"

McCarran hung his head and shuddered. Active thought he might start sobbing, but he collected himself.

"I still can't believe that she's...it's crazy that she's...Was it a robbery? Or, no, not a rape?"

"It was a brutal killing, too violent to be anything but personal."

"Personal? That doesn't make sense. Who would want to kill Shay?"

"You tell me, Josh. You wanted her to meet your family. Sounds like you invested your heart in her. And then she goes running back to Kim and dumps you by text."

"You think I did it? Me?" Sweat sheened his brow. "No way. After she called it quits, I never saw her again. As far as I knew, she was with Kim until she rotated back to the Slope. Why don't you ask that bitch what happened to her after I left?"

"For Anchorage?"

"Yes. I was there my whole two weeks. You can check with my roommate down there." McCarran picked up his phone and tapped up a contact. "He's a plumber. Here's his number."

Active took it down. "But, just to be clear, you went with Shalene to Chukchi, she went to Kim's, and you never saw her again?"

"Like I said, I waited for her at the airport but she never showed up. Then finally, she texted me to stay away and that's what I did."

"And you didn't text her again to ask why?"

"No."

He scrolled again on his phone, then tapped the screen with his thumb. "Here, see?"

He passed over the phone and Active studied the screen. The "OMW" text was followed by a two-part message:

i'm sorry, josh. i didnt mean for it to happen

like this. kim and i talked and I realize that shes the one i really love. I know I hurt you, but I CAN'T LIVE A...

...LIE. I hope that one day you can forgive me. PLEASE DO NOT contact me or try to see me

"I need photos of those," Active said.

"No problem."

Active took the shots with his phone, then noted down the times. "So you read that message, you get on the plane, and you leave? Just like that?"

"I couldn't think of anything to say, so I waited for TSA to fix their computers and the flight and left for Anchorage around 4:45."

"Did you think about trying to find her, ask her to her face why she decided to stay with Kim?"

"Yeah, but I didn't. I couldn't."

"Why is that?"

"Because she was with Kim. I didn't want to get into a confrontation. And I figured it'd be pointless anyway."

Active scribbled on his notebook, tapped it a couple of times like he was thinking, putting the pieces together, and let the silence build.

"Okay, I did think about it, but I didn't know where Kim lived," McCarran said.

Active raised an eyebrow. McCarran had introduced his lack of information about Kim's address without being asked. People did that when they had something to hide, explaining an issue before it came up, trying to head off the cop. Sometimes it was a false tell. But usually not.

"Come on, Josh. I think you knew exactly where Kim lived. I think Shalene told you before she took off to pick up her things."

"No." McCarran's voice was less emphatic now. His eyes rabbited around the room like he was chasing down his next words.

Active glanced at his notes and tapped the pad with his pen. "Shalene texted 'OMW' at 12:07. Her text telling you she was staying with Kim didn't come in until 1:16. I think within that hour of her not showing up, you got more and more pissed off, and instead of texting her again about where she was, I think you went to Kim's house and tried to talk to Shalene, to give her hell about keeping you waiting."

"Okay," McCarran said in a lower voice. "You're right. Shay did tell me where Kim's house was. I did go up there. I banged on the door and asked to see her. Kim wouldn't let me in. And then I got the text from Shay saying she was staying with Kim."

"That must have really set you off."

"I couldn't believe it at first, I read it over a couple of times. And, yeah, I was really pissed then. I started pounding on the door, cursing and yelling for Shay to come out."

"Did she answer?"

"No. Kim said Shay didn't want to talk to me, and if I didn't leave, they'd call the cops."

"That scared you off?"

"Yeah, it did. I was kind of acting like a crazy person, so yeah." McCarran ran his hand over his eyes. "I got into some trouble when I was in high school. My girl and I got into a beef and I was charged with assault. That's why I gave up and left. I didn't want to get caught up in anything like that again."

"What time did you leave Kim's place?"

McCarran stroked his beard. "I waited around at the airport for maybe twenty-five minutes after Shay said she was on her way, then I went to Kim's to find her. It wasn't much of a walk, but I took a wrong turn and had to backtrack a little. I didn't stick around there long, so I must have left a few minutes after the second txt, I guess. Close to one-thirty."

"You still had several hours before your flight. What did you do?"

"I walked around town for maybe a couple of hours, trying to get my head together."

"By yourself?" Active asked.

"Yeah, I didn't know anyone in Chukchi other than Shay. And Kim."

"Where did you go?"

"Down along this road past the airport to a beach area," McCarran said. "There were some tents and shacks down there like camps or something."

"Yeah, Tent City, they call it. Chukchi people have fish camps down there, people come in from the villages upriver and stay part of the summer for the chum salmon run, that kind of thing."

"Sounds right. I wouldn't really know."

"Right. You're a big city guy."

McCarran halfway grinned and shook his head. "Not all the time. I like the outdoors."

"Are you a hunter?"

"Are you kidding? My grandfather is Dusty McCarran."

"Dusty McCarran?"

"One of the most famous guides in Alaska? There are books about him, he's in Boone and Crockett," McCarran said. "I've gone hunting with Granddad since I was a kid. I could bring down a moose and field dress a caribou by the time I was eight."

"Interesting."

"You said Shay's death was brutal. How was she killed?"

"Sorry, I can't discuss that," Active said. "I'll be in touch."

In the airport shuttle, Active looked over the paperwork the company had provided. Personnel files for Shalene Harvey and three employees from Chukchi—Kim Tulimaq and two men named Banks.

Something tugged at the corner of his mind. What had he forgotten? Maybe it would come to him after a decent night's sleep.

Meantime, there was legwork to be done. He brought up Danny Kavik's contact on his phone and tapped it.

"Danny, I need you to check out a few things. We need Shalene's phone records, at least from May." He read the number off her file. "And run a background check on Joshua P. McCarran. I've texted you his DOB and the contact info for his roommate in Anchorage. We need to verify his alibi for the last half of May, also the alibi for a guy named Larry Hayden. He was supposedly staying with his sister in Fairbanks from May second through the end of the month. I'll text you her name and number, too."

"On it," Kavik said. "Anything else?"

"Yes. You know a Kim Tulimaq, or Randolph and Phillip Banks?"

"The Banks brothers, sure, I saw them just yesterday at E-Z Market. Pretty harmless, actually kinda nerdy by Chukchi standards—more into video games than hunting and fishing, as I recall. Kim Tulimaq I kinda knew in high school. She was a couple of grades behind me. She dressed like a boy, captain of the girls' basketball team. We all figured she was gay but I never really knew."

"If something jogs your memory, let me know. I need to talk to her when I get back."

"Right, and when is that?"

"Maybe tonight, otherwise tomorrow. I just remembered one more loose end."

He rang off and started negotiations with the shuttle driver for a quick detour back to the NES headquarters.

Fred Sullivan looked up from his desk in surprise when Active walked in.

"Chief Active. You're back. Something else we can do for you?"

Active scanned the bank of photos behind Sullivan, the photos of employee get-togethers he had seen on his first visit, until he spotted the one that had been tugging at his memory.

"That right there." Active pointed to a big photo of about thirty employees decked out in Mexican garb. "What is that?"

"This year's Cinco de Mayo party."

"When was it taken?"

"We have it as close to May fifth as we can, but at the shift rotation so the maximum number of employees can be here to enjoy it. This year it was May fourteenth. See, right there in the corner?"

Active looked closer and pointed at a woman near the center. She held a red rose between her teeth and wore a ruffled dress. "That's Shalene Harvey."

"Yep."

"And that's Josh McCarran." He moved his finger to a

figure in a green sombrero and a striped serape standing next to Shalene.

"Right."

"And who's this?" Active pointed to a young Native woman, three people down from McCarran, in a bright, flowered outfit. She was wiry, compact, and giving Josh and Shalene the side-eye.

"That's Kim Tulimaq."

Active waved his hand over the photo. "And these are all people who might have worked with Shalene the last time she was on the Slope?"

"Yes. Do you think the photo would help with your investigation?"

Active pulled out his phone and tapped the camera app to life. "Possibly. Mind if I get a picture of it?"

"I'll go you one better." Sullivan lifted the photo off the wall. "You can have it."

"Thanks, Mr. Sullivan. Oh, and I'll need Kim Tulimaq's file, too."

"You bet. Whatever we can do to help. I'm sure every single person in that picture would want justice for Shalene."

"Maybe not every single one," Active muttered to himself as he tucked the photo into his backpack.

CHAPTER TEN

·*August 27* ·

CHUKCHI

The Tahoe crunched on the gravel shoulder of Caribou Avenue as Active pulled to a stop in front of Kim Tulimaq's house at the northeast corner of Chukchi. It was a T1-11 plywood box set on wooden pilings with a small *qanichaq* on the front and more vacant lots than houses around.

A Yamaha four-wheeler, yellow except for a red front fender, was parked in the yard with a two-wheeled wooden trailer hitched on behind. Beside the house, a snowgo slept under a nylon cover with Arctic Cat markings.

The house was bright turquoise with yellow trim. A 500-gallon stove-oil tank on a wooden rack left of the *qanichaq* was painted in the same colors, with "USA" lettered on the side in white. Farther back was an outbuilding with a chimney that looked to be a sauna.

Two young cottonwoods hugged the east wall of the house, where the combination of light from the morning sun and shelter from Chukchi's relentless west wind actually let them thrive. Near one corner of the house stood a pair of sawhorses that looked like they needed something to hold up.

The lot was big by Chukchi standards and appeared to have included another house at some point. A jumble of timbers and a sheet of tin roofing lay in a heap toward the rear of the property.

Active went through the *qanichaq* and knocked on the inner door. He noted a rifle leaning in the corner of the arctic entry and a couple of nested plastic buckets, like the ones Grace used for berry picking. A pair of extension cords was looped over a big nail, a fox pelt hung by the nose from another one, and a set of shelves with tools and odds and ends of outdoor gear stood near the inner door. A standard Chukchi *qanichaq*, where things went that had no other place to go.

An Inupiat woman with a deep tan answered his knock. The scowl in the photo from Fred Sullivan's office was gone, but its replacement was a careful smile under deep black eyes that were also careful. She wore jeans and a cropped T-shirt. Her dark hair was cut short.

Active caught the aroma of baking, a mix of warm butter and sugar and maybe almond. His mouth watered as he introduced himself and said, "May I come in?"

"You're here about Shay." Tulimaq waved him in and closed the door, stone-faced now. She didn't offer him a seat, so they stayed at the door.

"You've heard then?"

"Everybody has. It's on Kay-Chuck. I was hoping they were wrong about the ID, but it's true, isn't it? She's dead."

"Yes."

Tulimaq slumped and put her hands over her eyes. "*Arii,* I knew something like this would happen if she went off with that guy. I should have stopped her. I knew he was trouble."

"What guy?"

"Josh McCarran." A burnt smell wafted in from the kitchen. "My cake! Hang on."

She hurried to the kitchen, threw open the oven, grabbed mitts, and pulled out a cake pan.

Active settled onto a pale yellow couch with only a single duct-tape patch, also yellow. He took out his notebook and studied the room. A scarred office desk stood in the corner with no clutter on top, only a closed laptop, a phone and a tablet, all plugged in and charging, all squared up with the edges of the desk.

The whole place gave off the same air of order and care. Neat, amazingly little dust despite the gravel streets and ceaseless winds of Chukchi, a small collection of prints on the walls. Landscapes, mostly, mountains and lakes in muted shades. And the cleanliness. The wood floor shone, the caribou skull over the door gleamed titanium white.

"Everything okay?" he asked as Tulimaq came back around the counter.

She dropped into a hard-back armchair and nodded. "Shay was the cook, which was fine with me. I did the cleaning."

"You said she left with Josh McCarran?"

She raised her eyebrows in the Inupiat *yes*. "When we were on R&R in May. She came here and then she left to go to Anchorage with him. I wanted her to stay, but, *arii*, that girl, there was no telling her anything if she made up her mind. If he didn't talk her into leaving, she would still be alive."

"Shalene would come here on R&R? She was from Nome, right?"

"We would spend our time off here. We'd been together about seven months, maybe. Ever since we hooked up at the company Halloween party. We had our bumps along the way, but I thought we would work it out."

"Bumps?"

"The normal things, little disagreements couples have. We're the same as straight people that way."

"Disagreements about what?"

"Work schedules, housecleaning, not enough sex, too much sex."

"Too much sex? That's possible?"

She didn't crack a smile and shot him a "don't bother" look.

"Our moods didn't always sync up."

"Any serious arguments, jealousy?"

"Not really," Tulimaq said. "Ah, sometimes, she would say some girl was hot, or even some guy, but she was just teasing. It was no big deal. When R&R came around, I knew she'd be coming back here with me. At least till he showed up."

"Josh."

She raised her eyebrows, *yes*, but didn't speak.

"So he enters the picture, he talks her into going to Anchorage with him." Active paused and doodled in his notebook. "How does that work exactly? Can a woman just change teams like that?"

"We don't call it teams."

"Point taken. But can she?"

Tulimaq's face took on a haunted look. "Not me, but some women can, and Shay wanted us to take a break while she worked it out. She kind of went back and forth between me and Josh for a couple of months. Then it was mostly Josh."

She paused, then shook her head and misted up.

"She told me she never really considered herself a lesbian, she just happened to fall in love with a woman."

"Ah."

Tulimaq was silent for a time, then cleared her throat. "And I was that woman. *Yoi,* so lucky."

"So if the two of you were breaking up, why was she here in May?"

"Josh was going to take her away to Anchorage. He even gave her some kind of cheap ring. I guess that was his way of sealing the deal." She rolled her eyes. "Shay told him she wanted to come up here to say good-bye to me and get her stuff from my house. He came along to make sure she didn't change her mind."

"And she didn't?"

"Didn't what?"

"Change her mind."

"No. She came to my place to get her stuff. She was gonna take it to the airport on my four-wheeler and meet Josh there to go to Anchorage. I asked her if she was sure she wanted to do it. 'Maybe you could give it more time,' I said. 'Don't rush into it.' But he wouldn't let her have any time."

"What do you mean, he wouldn't let her?"

"He was texting her, telling her the flight was delayed, badgering her, asking was she on her way. Stressing her out. He was so controlling. I could definitely see him getting violent with her. He beat up this old guy Larry at work."

"Is that why you threatened to call the cops when he came to your house?"

"What? No. He never came here."

"He didn't pound on your door, demanding for Shalene to come out?"

"No way," Tulimaq said. "He might be an asshole, but he's not stupid. I don't shoot to kill polar bears, but everybody on the Slope knows I could drop any animal with one shot, no problem. Including a two-legged one."

"So you didn't tell McCarran that Shalene didn't want to talk to him, didn't threaten to call the cops if he didn't leave?"

"*Arii*, why do you keep asking that? I already told you he was never here. And why wouldn't Shay talk to him if he was? She was about to go off with him. I asked her over and over was she sure until she stomped out with the last of her stuff and left on my four-wheeler."

"How did you get it back?"

"I walked down the next morning and got it from the airport."

"What time was that?"

"I couldn't sleep, I left here maybe four-thirty, five. I was home an hour later, or forty-five minutes maybe."

"Go anywhere else after you picked it up? Ride down the beach to clear your head, maybe?"

"No, I just came home. I needed some down time after...you know."

"Anybody see you pick it up at the airport?"

"*Arii*, I don't know. There's always people around there. But I didn't talk to anybody that I can remember."

"Did you ever hear from Shalene or see her again?"

"Never."

He scribbled on his pad. "So, what did you think when she didn't show back up at work?"

"I thought maybe she switched shifts. So I asked around but nobody had seen her. I figured Josh made her quit to keep her away from me." She twisted a ring on her left hand.

"It's not like I was going to ask him."

"That ring there." Active pointed with his pen. "Is that something special?"

Tulimaq let go of the ring and clasped her hands in her lap. "*Arii.*"

Active leaned in for a look and Tulimaq put out her hand. The ring was a thick sterling band with thin black curlicues worked into the silver. "That's some nice scrollwork."

"Shay gave it to me."

"And did you give her one?"

"Just like it, we bought them together." She spread her fingers to show the pattern. "See how the designs intertwine? It's supposed to stand for never-ending love. But I didn't see it on her finger anymore after she started seeing Josh. Funny, ah?"

"Do you know what happened to it?"

"He probably made her throw it away."

"But you still wear yours even after she dumped you for him?"

"I guess I'm not ready to let go."

"It must have been rough to see her with Josh. You were together for seven months. She stayed with you when you were off-shift. Your relationship was building, right?"

Tulimaq raised her eyebrows.

"Then, Josh shows up, puts a cheap ring on her finger, she throws yours away, and off she goes. And you just let her?"

Tulimaq's face contorted with anguish. "*Arii,* what was I gonna do? I said I tried to get her to stay. I told her he wasn't a good guy. But she was like a stubborn little kid that won't listen."

"That had to make you mad."

Tulimaq stayed quiet, lips pressed together and quivering slightly, chin puckered.

"So you're standing here in this room and she's telling you it's over, she wants Josh instead of you?"

"Yes." Tulimaq tipped her head at a corner. "Right there by the woodstove."

"It's understandable how you could lose it for a moment, get physical with her."

"Never! I wouldn't do that. Is that what you think? *Arii*, I - -"

"Or maybe it was her. Maybe she hit you first." Active shook his head. "These quiet homebody types, you never know. I mean, you would have a right to defend yourself."

Tulimaq's eyes widened. "You do think I hurt her!" Her eyes filled. "No, I loved her! I thought she was the one." She pulled up her T-shirt and swiped at the tears, then dabbed her nose. "Anyway, it was him that killed her. It has to be! She went off with him and now she's dead! Why you saying all this to me?"

Active glanced at his notebook. "When Shalene left for the airport to meet Josh, was she wearing the ring he gave her?"

Her eyes narrowed and her lips compressed to an angry line. "Yes, she had it on. You didn't find it with her...when you...where she..."

"No, not yet."

"He probably took it back to Target for his ten-dollar refund after he..." Tulimaq teared up and bit down on a knuckle.

"That's it? Anything else you need to tell me?"

Tulimaq was silent, head lowered in thought. "Not that I can remember. I think I - - no, there's nothing else."

"Well, here's the thing." Active reached for his phone. Tulimaq seemed to tense up.

"Josh says she never came to the airport. In fact, she texted him she decided to stay here with you." He brought up the text and turned the screen to face her. "See?"

"What?" She grabbed for the phone.

He jerked it back and pushed her hand away. "Don't do that, just read it."

She leaned in and absorbed the text for several seconds. Then, "Ohhhhh, noooooooo," she keened.

The sound was so loud and went on for so long that Active covered his ears to wait it out. Finally the keening trailed off into sobs and she collapsed on the sofa. He passed her his handkerchief. She blew her nose and handed it back.

"Ms. Tulimaq - -"

"She-huh, she-huh, she must have been on her way back to me! She sent him that text and he went after her and he killed her! I wanted us to get married someday but he came along and took her away and then she changed her mind and now he killed her! You huh-huh-have to arrest him!"

Active watched as she wiped tears on her sleeve, and watched him.

"Actually," he said, "maybe it's you I should arrest. That text could mean she never even went to the airport. Maybe she was here with you all along like Josh says. Maybe she sent him the text like he says, then she changed her mind one more time and tried to go to the airport and leave with him after all. But you couldn't let her go."

Active paused.

Tulimaq was shaking her head and mumbling "No, no, no." She got off the sofa and fumbled for the phone on the desk.

"Or, no, wait!" Active said with sudden inspiration. "Or maybe she didn't even send that message. Maybe you sent it with her phone after you killed her."

"No, no, no." Tulimaq was back on the sofa now, sobbing. "Look, see, she texted me from the airport with Josh." She brought up a text on the phone, held it out.

Active studied the message.

at the airport with josh. keys in the tailpipe. i know I made the right choice going with him. IF YOU CARE ABOUT ME PLEASE respect my decision. I'm sorry if...

...i hurt you

Active pulled out his phone to mask his astonishment and brought up the camera. "Mind if I get a photo of that?"

"No," she said, calmer now. "Why would I?"

He snapped the picture, then scrolled up and down to check for additional texts. There was just the one.

Then it dawned on him how little the new text meant.

"Or," he said, "you could have sent both texts after Shalene was dead."

"But I didn't! If anybody sent a text with her phone, it must be Josh!"

Active ran the scenario through his head and realized it was equally plausible.

He studied the supposed airport text from Shalene. "You didn't delete this, even after three months? It must have been very painful, having it on your phone."

"I did all her others, but that one I just couldn't. Somebody that big in your life, you don't want to let your last memory go, even if they're gone." She put her head down and twisted the silver ring again. *"Arii,* it would be like chipping off a piece of my heart."

"I'm sorry for your loss."

He waited a few moments and tried a change of subject. "Nice caribou skull up there. Your kill?"

"Sure."

"You hunt a lot?"

"I'm a Chukchi girl, so..."

"Right. Have you always lived here?"

"A long time. I lived with my *aana* here when I was a kid."

"Lots of village kids are raised by their *aanas,* all right. Is she doing well?"

Tulimaq gave a hint of a smile. "Millie Tulimaq is a tough old lady."

"Your father's mother?"

"No, my mom's. She was from Chukchi."

Active noted that Kim used her mother's family name. Perhaps her parents weren't married. "Was?"

"She died from cancer when I was thirteen."

"And your dad?"

"He was from Nuliakuk. We lived up there after my mom passed. Then he and my stepmom died a year later, and I came to Chukchi to stay with my *aana.*"

"You lost your mom, then your dad and your stepmom so soon after that? That had to be rough."

"Our house burned down. They died in the fire. Somebody found me outside in the shed."

"Sorry if I brought up another bad time in your life."

She wiped her eyes on her T-shirt. "It's okay. It was a long time ago. Could I just be alone now? You coming here like this, it brings up all my times with Shay."

"Hey, Boss," Danny Kavik looked up from Fred Sullivan's Cinco de Mayo photo as Active returned to his office. "How was Kim Tulimaq?"

"It's complicated."

"What?"

Active dropped into his chair and took Kavik through the interview, then showed him the dueling texts on his phone and told him about the dueling scenarios.

"Jesus!"

"Exactly. This thing is like a Rubik's cube."

Kavik scrolled back and forth between the texts. "So the times here, they - -"

"Yeah, they line up with what Kim said. The one to her from Shalene was at 12:27, when she would have been back at the airport with Josh. And the one to Josh was thirty-nine minutes later, at 1:16, enough time for Shalene to change her mind, and for him to kill her and still have a couple hours to dispose of the body before catching his plane out that afternoon."

"Huh," Kavik said. "Do we buy it?"

"On the other hand, if Kim killed Shalene when she first tried to leave for the airport she would have had her phone all the while and could have sent both texts."

"And that fits the timeline, too."

Both men were silent for several seconds.

Finally Active spoke. "Kind of a tossup, all right. Who do you like?"

"Right now? Him, I guess."

"Me, too," Active said. "I mean he did admit to being down in Tent City, he was evasive and defensive, he hedged a few times. Whereas, Kim...her story just to come straight out of her, you know?"

"Yep."

"Obviously, we need to track that phone. I guess the phone company in Nome is our only hope."

"On it," Kavik said.

"And I guess we need to get Procopio to subpoena all of their phone companies for the texts any of them sent or received starting, when, three months before the murder?"

Kavik started to protest.

Active raised a hand. "Yeah, it took eight weeks the last time we had to do that. But if we don't figure this out by then, we'll be - -"

"Yeah, in cold case mode." Kavik made a note. "But if we do reach that point, maybe we can find some kind of expert on text analysis to tell us which one of them sent the fake messages from Shalene's phone?"

"Can't hurt to try, I suppose. But God, I hope it doesn't come to that." Active turned the case over in his head for a few moments, running down his mental to-do list one more time.

"Let's check out the Banks brothers," Active said. "And have a couple of guys canvass Tulimaq's neighbors, would you? Maybe somebody saw McCarran up there raising hell that day."

"Be a long shot after so much time, but sure." Kavik made more notes.

He dropped his eyes to the Cinco de Mayo photograph that lay between them on Active's desk blotter.

"Spot something new in there?" Active asked.

"Not really. Josh and Shalene look happy enough, holding hands. And Kim looks unhappy enough. About what you'd expect in a love triangle."

"Hold on a sec," Active said. He dug his loupe out of a desk drawer and put it over the image of Shalene in the photo. The resolution wasn't great, but what he was looking for came through clearly enough.

"Check it out," he said. "She's definitely wearing a ring."

Kavik bent over the loupe and took a look. "Just like Kim said."

"And on the same finger that got cut off."

"Somebody really cared about that ring," Kavik said.

"Yep."

"So. What next?"

"I'm going back up to the Slope to see what Josh has to say for himself now that we've got Kim's text. Oh, yeah—did you reach his roommate?"

"Yeah, he says McCarran was in Anchorage for his entire R&R following his flight back from Chukchi. The roommate actually picked him up from the airport that night."

"So he left Chukchi when he said he did." Active studied McCarran's face in the photo. "But a good liar always wraps his lies in the truth."

CHAPTER ELEVEN

· August 28 ·

DEADHORSE, PRUDHOE BAY

Active found Josh McCarran at a two-seat corner table in the cafeteria at North Slope Environmental. He was at work on a plate piled with salmon filets, white bread, and baked beans topped with bacon slices. He didn't look up until Active settled into a chair with one short leg that made it rock when he shifted his weight.

"Jesus," McCarran said. "You working up here now?"

"Nope, just wanted to have another chat if we could."

McCarran gave a resigned roll of the eyes. "Want something?" he said around a mouthful of the beans. "Coffee?"

"No thanks."

The cafeteria was set up like most, with bins of steaming entrees, salad and dessert sections, and a beverage dispenser at the end of a long stainless-steel rail. But on the Slope the entrees included filets of king salmon, slabs of beef brisket and rib-eye steak, potatoes cooked every way they could be, and cakes that looked like they came out of a gourmet pastry shop.

Active had heard from Slope workers that the food was

109

one of the perks that helped make up for the isolation and brutal climate. Most of them seemed to end up with big bellies to match their big beards. McCarran had the beard but not the belly. Maybe he just hadn't been at it long enough.

Two young Native men hunched over their meals at one of the square, wooden tables. Four older white guys worked their way down the serving line, talking, belly-laughing, and swearing as they loaded up.

"So what's this about?" McCarran said. "I told you what I knew last time. You talked to my roommate in Anchorage, right?"

"Correct. But we still need to fill in some gaps."

"Gaps?" McCarran had scarfed up half of the food on his tray. He wiped his lips with a balled-up napkin and dabbed at the tips of his mustache. "Sure, anything you need."

"The last time we talked you said Shalene texted you she was on her way to the airport and when she didn't show up, you went by Kim's house. You banged on the door and left after Kim threatened to call the cops."

McCarran nodded and mopped up bean broth with a chunk of bread.

"Then, according to our last talk, you walked around town for a couple of hours before the plane left for Anchorage."

"Right." McCarran stuffed the soaked bread into his mouth. "I needed to clear my head."

"Where did you walk?"

"I told you that already."

"Tell me again. I want to make sure I have it right."

"Well, down past the airport like I said, around - - what did you call it, Tent City?"

"Uh-huh. You see anybody down there, talk to anybody?"

"No. There might have been a couple people around, but I kept my distance." McCarran finished his plate and pushed the tray to the center of the table. "You know, strange white guy in a Native village, you don't walk up on people."

"You go inside any of the camps and shacks out there? Maybe explore some of them?"

"No. I wasn't exactly in the mood for exploring."

"Where did you go after Tent City?"

"Back to the airport and caught the plane to Anchorage."

"How much time did you spend in Tent City? Two hours you said?"

"Uh, not that long. Maybe an hour or less. Forty-five minutes at the most. I was worried about getting back to the airport in case they got the computers fixed quicker than they said."

"Are you sure you didn't hang around Tent City longer than forty-five minutes?"

Active concentrated on his notes again and let McCarran stew. The Sloper's foot started to tap under the table.

"No. I had already burned up some time going to Kim's and trying to see Shay. I didn't want to miss my flight."

Active arched an eyebrow. "Come on, Josh."

"What?"

"Stop yanking my chain. You never went to Kim's house."

"Of course I did, I told you already. Shalene didn't come to the airport, so I went up there - -"

McCarran stumbled to a halt as Active pulled out his phone, brought up the text to Kim, and slowly rotated the screen to face him.

"That's not what Shalene said." Active waited as McCarran scanned the text. "At the airport, she said. With you. You see that?"

"That's bullshit! She never came to the airport!"

Heads turned and the Slopers in the cafeteria stared at the two of them, then turned away at the sight of Active's uniform.

Active gave McCarran a moment, then continued. "And a half hour after that, she tells you she's decided to go back to Kim and three months later we find her body in Tent City. Where you admit going. You can see how it looks."

"I don't care how it looks, she never came to the damned airport. They must have video in the terminal, did you check that? That'll show she was never there!"

"We are checking but they only have it at the TSA station. So her not showing up on it wouldn't necessarily mean she was never in the terminal."

Active paused and waited. McCarran didn't speak. He just stared at the text.

"Or maybe she never went in," Active said. "Maybe you meet her outside when she shows up on Kim's four-wheeler, she sends that text to Kim, and then the two of you take a walk together or maybe a ride on the four-wheeler. So you're down in Tent City, like you said, she changes her mind, you have a fight, she starts back to town by herself and sends you that text saying to leave her alone. And you lose it. You can't stand the idea she'd rather have a woman in her bed than you. So you chase her down and kill her."

McCarran shook his head and slapped the table. "This is total bullshit, dammit! All I know is, she went to Kim's house and I never saw her again, at the airport or anywhere else. I did go to Tent City, but I went alone and I didn't go in any old shacks and I didn't kill anybody."

"Look. She sent you and Kim basically identical texts

saying she was leaving each of you for the other. What the hell was going on?"

"How the fuck do I know? Maybe there was someone else she was, I don't know, involved with that I didn't know about?"

"You expect me to believe she was playing both of you for someone else altogether? And this mystery lover killed her? Come on."

"She was a woman," McCarran said. "They...well, you know. You can never be sure of anything with a woman."

"All right," Active said. "Just one more thing."

McCarran stood up with his empty tray. "I gotta get back to my shift," he said. "I don't want to lose my job."

"Did Shalene give you back the ring?"

McCarran recoiled. "How do you know about the ring?"

"I'm a cop is how. You might want to keep that in mind."

McCarran shook his head, as if to clear it. "No, I didn't get the ring back because I didn't see her, like I told you."

"Describe that ring for me, please."

"It was a plain silver band. I was going to get her something fancier when things moved farther along. I didn't want to crowd her. Why you asking me this? Wasn't it on her when you found her?"

"No." Active locked his eyes onto McCarran's. "But I expect it'll turn up." Active watched for a tell. McCarran didn't flinch.

"All I know is, it was on her finger when she went up to Kim's. Maybe if she was gonna stay, she took it off."

McCarran turned and walked out of the cafeteria.

Active watched him go as he unmuted his phone and checked for traffic. No texts or voicemails, only a missed call from Kavik a few minutes earlier. Kavik, he decided, could wait. He had half an hour before the flight back to Chukchi, just enough time to swing by Fred Sullivan's office.

He recognized the Inupiat woman at the reception desk. She was the one who'd brought in the employee files on his last trip to Deadhorse. The human resources specialist, that was it.

"Molly, right?"

"Chief Active." She smiled and nodded. "Is there something else you needed?"

"Is Mr. Sullivan in?"

"No. He's out in the field until late this afternoon. Could I help you?"

"Maybe you can. I'm aware that Shalene Harvey filed a complaint against Larry Hayden a few months ago."

"Yes, we investigated that."

Active nodded. "Did Shalene file any complaints against anyone else?"

"Do you think she was killed because of a complaint?"

"We're not ruling anything out at this point."

Molly paused, shifted in her chair and arched her back.

"Are you all right?" Active asked.

"Baby's kicking." She grimaced, then relaxed. "You'd have to talk to Mr. Sullivan about employee complaints."

"Aren't you in HR? Wouldn't those come to you?"

"I don't want to say anything inappropriate. Mr. Sullivan would be the person to talk to." She looked down and began shuffling through a stack papers with what struck Active as feigned urgency. "I have to get these timesheets done, so..."

Push her on it, or hit on Sullivan again to find out what she was covering up?

He was about to assure her it was always appropriate to talk to the police when his cell phone buzzed and Kavik's ID came up. "Hey, Danny, sorry for not getting back to you, I'm still - -"

"We've finished processing the body site," Kavik said.

"Find anything interesting?"

"Depends."

Active listened as Kavik described the discovery.

"Jesus, that doesn't make any sense. Take photos but leave them where you found them. And put an officer on the site till I get there."

GHOST LIGHT

CHAPTER TWELVE

·August 28 ·

CHUKCHI

Kavik was waiting for Active at Lienhofer Aviation when the company's North Slope shuttle taxied in. As they bounced toward Tent City in Kavik's Tahoe, Active briefed him on the interview with Josh McCarran, including the Sloper's suggestion that Shalene might have had a third lover.

"So he's saying both of those texts actually were sent by Shalene and she was just kicking sand in everybody's eyes so she could run off with this...with this..."

"Right, with this magic killer who steps out of the shadows and solves everybody's problem except ours."

"Yeah," Kavik said. "What a load of horse...huh."

"What?"

"I mean, this girl. A male lover, a female lover, can we really rule out another one?"

"I guess not. But I don't buy it. Do you?"

"Not really," Kavik said as they pulled up at the old shack in Tent City. "Too complicated. Usually it's simple."

Moments later, they were inside and Active was squatting on the cellar floor. He played his flashlight across the expanse of mud and gravel and patches of permafrost ice where Kavik pointed. The beam caught a glint of metal. Active brushed away a bit of dirt.

The plain silver band was wedged against the wall several feet from where they had found Shalene Harvey's butchered body. Active picked it up with a pen and studied it, then bagged it.

"Nice work," he told Kavik.

Kavik grimaced, as if to say it was nothing, finding this tiny ring in a cold, dark cellar. "You think it's the one she's wearing in that photo from the Slope?"

"Probably," Active said. "It does fit McCarran's description of the ring he gave her. But why's it so far from the body?"

"The killer took it off her and dropped it?"

"Or it got moved around by the scavengers. Or even by Tommie."

"Good point," Kavik said. "How *do* we know what the killer did and what Tommie did?"

"Fair question, but I'm doubting Tommie moved that ring. Old lady, probably with weak eyesight, wandering around in the twilight, it doesn't seem like she could have seen anything this small in a place this dark just with that little flashlight of hers."

"The other one's outside."

Kavik led the way out of the shack to a grassy clearing out front. The area was sectioned off with string into one-foot quadrants, each marked with a small, numbered orange flag.

"Here it is." Kavik pointed to a square with a blue marker where the ground sloped down along a path to the beach. "Alan found it."

Active knelt and studied the spot. The mat of grass and moss had grown up around the ring since it was dropped and now it was barely visible. He pulled out his pen again and worked the ring with its intricate scrollwork up and out of the vegetation. He rose and held out the ring on the pen. "This I've seen before."

"How - -"

"On Kim Tulimaq's finger. She has one just like it."

Kavik let out a low whistle. "Two rings, two lovers. That's the first verse of a country song right there."

"Plus there's murder," Active said. "For the chorus, maybe."

He bagged the ring, then looked at the alders and tundra around them. "But why would it be outside the house like this?"

"Dropped on the way in? Or out?"

"But who by? Georgeanne said that finger was probably cut off to remove a ring. But which ring? This one or the one Josh gave her?"

"And those texts," Kavik said. "Who - -"

"For my money," Active said, "the killer has to have sent at least some of those texts, maybe all of them. If it was Josh, then Shalene would have sent that first text saying "OMW," and the next one saying she was at the airport with him, which was true. Then he killed her and sent the third text to himself saying she had decided to stay with Kim. That would point the finger at her and mess with us if the body ever turned up."

"Which, you have to admit, does seem to be working."

Active gave him a sour look and continued. "But if Kim was the killer, she has to have sent all the fake texts—the "OMW" text, the second one to herself supposedly from Shalene at the airport, and the third one to Josh where Shalene supposedly said she had decided to stay with Kim after all."

"Which left Kim in a perfect position to say that was why Josh killed Shalene, because she changed her mind and was coming back to Kim," Kavik said. "Which would also mess with us if the body turned up, and which, again, does seem to be - -"

Active had raised his hand. "Stop saying that. Can we just stipulate, everything the killer is doing is working so far, unlike anything we're doing?"

Kavik grinned. "Yes, Boss."

Active grinned back. "And don't say that either." He chewed his lip for a moment, then waved at the shack. "No cell phone in there, I take it?"

"No such luck," Kavik said. "But that reminds me--I did get hold of the Nome phone company. We also struck out on the location data. She had one of those cheap little flip-phones that only does calls and text, none of your fancy smart-phone stuff like GPS or maps or Facebook. And they can't triangulate her phone that day because we've only got the one cell tower up here."

"Our luck," Active said.

"Oh, yeah. And there's more good news. We struck out with Kim Tulimaq's neighbors. To quote what one of 'em said, '*Arii*, that girl is always running around on that four-wheeler. Who knows what she was doing back in May?'"

"And the Banks brothers?"

"Ditto," Kavik said. "Both on the Slope all through the middle of May."

Active shook his head and waved Alan Long over from his post near the sagging *qanichaq* door on the old house. "Nice work spotting that ring in the grass there, Alan."

Long, whom Active had inherited with the job upon

ow she looked good, about her breasts
d she wear panties. What was creepy was
they were from someone who was
ast one said, 'I'd like to visit you when
in the cafeteria.' Shalene was really

could have been working the same shift?
ea who it was?"

no name except it was a gmail address
omeoRick.' I checked all of our personnel
ck three years. We've never had any
Romeo, but we've had three Richards, one
kys. I can send the information to your

d thanks. Did Shalene answer any of the

ot."

hem?"

re three. I'll send them, too."

great."

?" Her voice was steadier now.

to say you got this from me?"
so," Active said. "I'll do what I can."
and briefed Kavik on the call.
said. "Another admirer."
e said. "The third lover McCarran was

this girl. What did she have?"
up the copy of Harvey's ID photo on his
ed the hazel eyes and crooked, sunny smile.
ll start on the legwork when we get the

124

---

becoming chief of Chukchi Public Safety, was round faced, bucktoothed, enthusiastic, and barely good enough to keep on the force. Except once in a while when he outdid himself, and this was one of those whiles. The round face was split by a big smile.

"Thanks, Chief! It was nothing!"

Over Long's shoulder, Active saw Kavik roll his eyes.

"So, listen." Active handed Long the two rings. "You take these up to the office and put them in an evidence locker, okay?"

"You bet, Chief!" Long took the rings and headed for his Tahoe.

"Did you find anything else?" Active asked Kavik as Long pulled away.

"Just a little bone carving hidden in a crack in the wall."

"Carving of what?"

"See for yourself."

Kavik led him in and showed him the spot. Active worked the carving out of the wall with his pen and into an evidence bag. He held it up to the light and examined the tiny figurine of a whale-headed dog inside.

"Well, I'll be damned. That's a - -"

"That's exactly what it is," Kavik said.

"So this is what Tommie was looking for."

"Has to be."

Active shook the bag. "Does it look like evidence to you?"

"Nope. In fact, I'd happily swear in court I never saw it."

Active slipped the bag into his jacket pocket. "Saw what?"

They went back outside. Active swept his hand over the clearing in front of the shack. "No blood out here?"

"No blood, no sign of a struggle, just the ring."

121

"Which suggests she was killed somewhere else." Active stretched, still stiff after the flight from the Slope. "But where? McCarran didn't know the town, so, if he's our killer, where would he do it?"

"Somewhere else in Tent City? There's a lot of cover—all of these thickets, the various shacks and tents, and not a lot of folks around yet in mid-May."

"Let's say he did kill her down here," Active said. "And let's say he stabbed her with a hunting knife. Where would he get the knife? He couldn't have had it with him on the plane."

"Maybe it was in Shalene's stuff when she moved out of Kim's place? Fairly standard equipment if she and Kim spent a lot of time out in the country, right?"

"Correct," Active said. "And maybe even trash bags, too, if she was using them to round up her stuff as she packed. But let's not take anything for granted here. You check out the stores closest to the airport, ones that sell knives or trash bags. Look at the charge slips for May fifteenth and take Josh's photo with you. See if anyone remembers him."

"After three months?"

"A guy like Josh McCarran might register with a female sales clerk."

"Yeah, maybe we'll get lucky."

"But first," Active said, "it's time for another talk with Ms. Procopio. Get hold of her and see if she can get us warrants on Tulimaq's house, her four-wheeler, and the surrounding property."

"Roger that."

"And take me to Public Safety, if you would."

As they bounced through Tent City toward Chukchi, Active's phone went off. The prefix was 659, meaning a documents from Molly."

Kavik dropped him off at Public Safety, and he checked the time on his phone as he climbed into his own Tahoe. Almost five. Grace wouldn't be home from work for another hour. Maybe he'd drive along the beach, let the statements from Josh McCarran and Kim Tulimaq rattle around in his head. Maybe something would jump out at him, point the investigation in one direction or another. Any direction, actually, as long as it was one direction instead of three.

Two white swans glided across the porcelain blue sky just ahead. He rolled down the window to let in the cool, damp air. The burning sensation inched up his leg again. When was his next appointment with the Anchorage therapist?

Appointment! This was the day he had arranged for Kinnuk Landon to talk with Nelda Qivits. Now he had only fifteen minutes to swing by Landon's place near the airport and get him to Nelda's little cabin near the lagoon.

Six minutes later, Active pulled up at Landon's Conex and yelped the siren.

A Conex was solid metal, but someone had cut a squarish hole—apparently with a welding torch--in the side of this one and duct-taped Visqueen over it to make a window. Near the window, a stovepipe emerged through another cut-out, more or less circular, with fuzzy pink fiberglass insulation stuffed around the pipe to keep in the heat.

A face, hazy behind the Visqueen, appeared at the window, then vanished. In a moment, the steel door screeched open and Landon came out, Buster held to his chest with one hand, the other grasping a Budweiser and a big Ziploc of dried salmon strips. He set the salmon and beer on the Tahoe's fender, dropped Buster onto the passenger seat, returned to the Conex, and locked the door with a stainless-steel padlock.

"You know you can't have alcohol in here," Active said as Landon settled into the passenger seat.

Landon lowered his window and held the Budweiser outside. He put the salmon strips in a sweatshirt pocket.

"Those for Nelda?" Active asked.

"She like her Eskimo food, all right."

After that, Landon was silent and Active made no further attempt at conversation. Landon was in the vehicle and they were headed for Nelda's. That was enough.

The tribal healer swung her *qanichaq* door open before they could knock. She peered out through her old-school cataract glasses with their huge lenses, first at Active, then at Landon. She took the Bud from Landon's hand, grasped his wrist like a white doctor taking a pulse, and rattled off something in Inupiaq that Active couldn't catch.

Landon said "*Arii*" and disappeared into the cabin.

She turned the cataract lenses on Active. "You never understand that, ah, *naluaqmiiyaaq*?"

He shook his head, then remembered and squinted the Inupiat *no*.

"You should learn Inupiaq better." She emptied Landon's beer and handed Active the can. "I tell him, 'Bout time you come, ah?'"

"I hope you can help him. He's in trouble. And there's a girl who - -"

"I know about that girl, all right." She pointed at the sky. "She's up there and she want Kinnuk to help you catch that guy kill her."

"I sure want him to."

She raised her eyebrows, *yes*, then looked down at his aching leg and back into his eyes. "'Bout time you come see

126

would you?"

"On it," Kavik said as Active's phone screen lit up with another message, this time from Theresa Procopio.

"Got it," Kavik said a minute later. "He lives in Anchorage."

"At least I'm racking up the frequent-flyer miles."

"When you going?"

"I'll figure that out later." He showed Kavik the message from Procopio. "Right now, we have a great big beautiful search warrant for Kim Tulimaq's place."

When Active and Kavik drove up to the turquoise house a few minutes later, Kim Tulimaq was laying a sheet of plywood across the two sawhorses in the yard. It was the standard Chukchi rig for cleaning fish and carving up game without making a mess inside.

A five-gallon plastic bucket of chum salmon sat on the ground beside Tulimaq's Xtratuf boots. She scowled as Active handed her a printout of the search warrant and explained the reason for the visit.

"Got nothing to hide." She pulled a chum onto the plywood and slit the belly from anus to gills with a single quick, sure stroke.

The plywood was clean and dry except for where the fish guts spilled out. "New cutting board?" Active asked. "I don't think I saw it the last time I was here."

Tulimaq didn't look up as she finished filleting the fish, grabbed another out of the bucket, gutted it, and hacked off the head. "I keep it out back. It can get kind of messy."

"It doesn't look messy. Most of the ones I see around town are covered with fish guts and blood," Active said.

"Not mine. I like things clean."

Alan Long's Tahoe pulled up.

"Can you please put down the knife and step aside?" Active said. "Officer Kavik needs to get some photos and I'm going to need for you to hand over your phone to Officer Long here, and to stay with him while we conduct the search." He waved at Long as he climbed out of his vehicle. "And we're going to confiscate all the knives on the premises."

"For what?"

"To test for human blood."

"You're wasting your time."

Denial or challenge? Active wondered. Did she mean that she had nothing to do with Shalene's murder, or that she had covered her tracks too well for anything to be found?

He squatted beside the four-wheeler and examined every inch of it. Mud was caked on the wheels, but the worn seat and body were free of anything more interesting than dust.

When Active went inside, Kavik had already pulled items from the drawers and cupboard. It was the usual stuff: cheap dishes and mugs, mismatched silverware, bags of flour and sugar, a can of Crisco, bags of coffee beans, household cleaners, and two gallons of bleach.

Kavik tossed a box of fifty-five-gallon trash bags on the kitchen table. "What do you think?"

"They look like the ones the body was wrapped in, which means they're exactly like you'd find in every house in town, including mine."

"And mine," Kavik said.

Active surveyed the living room. The open area between the back of the sofa and the woodstove was about the only space big enough to butcher a body. A sheet of plywood the size of Kim's cutting board would fit easily. Georgeanne had said cutting a body up wouldn't necessarily be all that messy if it had been let lie a few hours for the blood to congeal. Still, the killer could have missed something in the cleanup. Killers usually did.

He knelt and crawled slowly along the edge of the tan-colored living room rug. Under a back leg of the couch, the border of the rug showed a patch of yellow-white, possibly from being bleached by accident while the floor was being cleaned. But so what? Maybe she used bleach on her floor even if she wasn't cleaning up after a murder. He photographed the spot, then sawed it out of the carpet with his belt knife and sealed it into an evidence bag.

"We might have something here," Kavik called from the kitchen. Active walked over as he scraped flakes of red-brown residue off the kitchen counter and into an evidence bag. "Blood, maybe?"

"Looks like," Active said. "Probably too recent to be Shalene's, but let's get it tested. She did stay here for a while and she was the cook, according to Kim. So she could have cut herself."

Kavik held up the bag and studied the flakes. "Or it could be animal blood."

"Fish, moose, caribou, who knows?" Active said. "Which is why we have the crime lab. Get some photos of that area behind the sofa while I check the bedrooms, okay?"

The house had two bedrooms, one devoted to storage. Cardboard cartons, some labeled, some not, were piled on the double bed with a black snowgo suit, two sleeping bags, and a tanned wolf hide. More boxes shared the closet with a row of serious winter parkas—heavily insulated, with ruffs of wolf fur—hanging from the rod and a stack of blankets on the shelf above.

He called Kavik in and they rifled through the

cartons. Books, snowgo parts, rifle cartridges, broken picture frames, an old landline telephone, even some Bibles and stuffed toys that Active surmised must have belonged to the previous tenant. But absolutely nothing of interest in the murder of Shalene Harvey.

In the other bedroom, a queen-sized bed took up most of the space. It was covered with a quilt in shades of green and brown appliquéd with bears and evergreen trees.

Over a small chest of drawers hung an oval mirror with photos stuck between the carved wooden frame and the edge of the glass. Kim and Shalene held up a huge sheefish in a springtime ice camp, they ate blueberry pie, they soaked in a hot spring surrounded by snow-covered trees. They sat on suitcases, one plain black, the other neon green with a miniature purple teddy bear the handle, in front of Chukchi's Alaska Airlines terminal. They made crazy faces with crossed eyes, flashed peace signs, grinned, and kissed. Glitter letters on the mirror spelled out "HAPPY TIMES."

Nothing in the room except the photos suggested two lovers once lived there. The drawers were filled with neatly folded jeans, T-shirts, and sweaters, all plain in style and all the same size. Jackets hung in the closet above a row of boots and sneakers. Everything was placed to take up the minimum amount of room. It seemed sad somehow. Shalene, it appeared, was the one who brought sparkle and perhaps a little happy chaos to the relationship.

"Anything interesting?" Active asked Kavik as he returned to the main living area.

Kavik was pushing the refrigerator back into place

against the wall, "Not much. I collected a few more knives, but that's it."

Active stared at a calendar on the wall beside the fridge. The photo for August showed a cow moose wading across a stream. Weeks were blocked off with pink and yellow highlighter. Active figured the colors represented Tulimaq's work shifts on the Slope and time off in Chukchi. Some of the dates bore scribbled notes: "3 pm, dentist," "pick up Ak Air cargo," and "stove oil delivery." Active flipped through the past months. Below another moose, this one a bull peering out of a stand of willows, May had only a single notation, for the fifteenth of the month: "Shalene arr--10:05."

"People still use those, huh?" Kavik said behind him. "I thought everybody put everything on their phones and computers now."

"It's not mutually exclusive, I guess. Did you find a laptop?"

"No such luck."

"Great. What we need is a record of what she was doing on the last days of Shalene's life."

"Well, they're Millennials," Kavik said. "Millennials can't brush their teeth without putting it on - -"

"--on social media, duh." Active shook his head. "And who's our very own queen of social media?"

"Lucy," Kavik said. "I'll get her on it."

GHOST LIGHT

CHAPTER FOURTEEN

·August 30 ·

ANCHORAGE

"You didn't have to come all this way." Fred Sullivan spoke from the doorway of the middle unit in a row of brown two-story condos. "We could have handled it by phone and you could have returned my photo by mail."

Active stood on the small porch under an arching branch of mountain ash heavy with red berries. The late-summer air was crisp and dry. A vee of southbound Canada geese arrowed overhead, their honks mixing with the traffic noise of midtown Anchorage. In Alaska, he reflected, winter was never really gone, just waiting over the northern horizon.

Down the street a garbage truck whirred and banged as it emptied a dumpster into its bed. Active handed Sullivan the Cinco de Mayo picture in a manila envelope. The Chihuahua he had seen on the Slope materialized between its owner's legs in a frenzy of yapping.

"Thanks for taking time for a few more questions." Active had to shout to make himself heard over the racket from the dog.

"Sure," Sullivan said. "Whatever I can do to help." He scooped up the Chihuahua with a hand under its belly. The dog continued to bark and added a snarl now that it was closer to Active's face. "Don't mind my Quita. Little dog with a big attitude, you know what I mean?"

He scratched Quita behind the ears. She stopped barking and licked his arm.

"You probably have to be when you weigh five pounds and live among Slopers in work boots," Active said.

Sullivan grinned. "Come on in, I'll put her in the bathroom. We'll have the place to ourselves. The wife's at bingo."

Active drew a notebook and pen from his jacket pocket as Sullivan waved him to the sofa and left with the dog.

The living room was Spartan, with pale walls that couldn't decide whether to be pink or orange and little sign of a woman's touch. Sullivan returned, dog-free, and squeezed himself into a chair a too small for his bulk.

Heavy, silky drapes were drawn back to let in a stream of late afternoon sun. Ivory carvings of walruses, seals, and seabirds were strewn across shelves and tables. A wedding photo was propped against a lamp on an end table. Sullivan posed with a short, chubby blonde woman, both fifteen years or so younger. He wore a suit, she a knee-length dress with a spray of flowers in her hair. There was no sign of children.

Active's gaze stopped on the wall across from the front window. Knives of various designs and sizes--hunting knives, daggers, even a sword in a gold and maroon scabbard—were displayed on silver brackets, blades glinting in the slanting sunlight.

Active pointed. "That's quite a collection."

"The sword I inherited from my father," Sullivan said. "He used to tell people it was from the Spanish-American War. Fact, fiction, who knows, but it's a good story. I've added the others over the years. I guess I have a thing about knives."

"A thing?"

"They're fascinating because they're both tools and weapons. And what else can do something as simple as slicing an apple and as serious as heart surgery?"

"Uh-huh. You ever use any of them?"

"Nope, those are strictly collectibles. The wife's not crazy about 'em, but they do make a great conversation piece."

Frantic whining and scratching erupted from the bathroom. Sullivan glanced at the door. "You said you had more questions?"

"Just a few," Active said. "You visit Chukchi much?"

Sullivan smiled stiffly and straightened a little. "No, no reason to, really."

"Did you have a reason in May?"

"May? Hm." Sullivan massaged his chin and made a show of trying to remember. "Not that I recall. May, you said?"

Active masked a smile. The thing about people who didn't lie much was, they weren't very good at it. Which you needed to be if you wanted to get something past a cop, because cops got lied to all the time. He cleared his throat.

"Yes, not too long after that photo was taken." Active nodded at the Cinco de Mayo photo he had laid out on the coffee table while Sullivan was sequestering Chiquita.

"No, I don't think so, no. But of course that was several months ago, so, you know ..."

"Maybe this will help." Active took out his phone and tapped the screen. He hit "send" and a swoosh sounded. "Check your e-mail."

Sullivan frowned, reached for his phone and scrolled down the screen. "Uh, I don't see any message. Probably have to give it a moment."

"I sent it to your personal address."

"Personal address?" Sullivan looked a little stunned. "But how did you - -"

"I'm a cop is how. You want to see if it's there?"

Sullivan frowned and checked his phone again. Beads of sweat glistened along his hairline. "Yeah, here it is."

"So 'RomeoRick.' That's you."

"Okay, So, you got my personal e-mail address somehow." Sullivan sounded irritated now. "What's this?"

"As you can see, the charge receipt from the Aurora Market attached to that e-mail shows you were in Chukchi on May sixteenth.

Sullivan stared at his phone and shifted in the chair. "Well, obviously, there's been some kind of mistake. I would have been off at the end of the month. I spend my time off here in Anchorage, as you can see."

"Any reason you would stop in Chukchi before coming to Anchorage?"

Sullivan slapped his forehead with the heel of his palm. Active had to mask another smile.

"Oh, yeah," Sullivan said. "That must have been the time I missed my flight on Alaska and I was gonna be stuck in Deadhorse an extra day. But a pilot buddy of mine was in town. He was headed to Nome so he offered to drop me off in Chukchi and I caught Alaska from there to Anchorage that night. I forgot all about it."

"Was Shalene on that flight?"

"No, I think she left the day before."

"Did you happen to see her while you were in Chukchi?"

"I only went there to make the connection to Anchorage. Why would I see Shalene?"

"It seems you were kind of interested in her."

"Interested? She was my employee so of course I was interested in her well-being, like I am with any employee."

"So it was her well-being you were thinking of when you sent her those personal e-mails?"

Sullivan shifted in the chair again. "Personal? What e-mails? I don't know what you're talking about."

Active laid his notebook and pen aside and leaned in on Sullivan as he read from his phone: "'Shalene, you looked good in those tight black pants this morning. Did you wear those for me?'"

He paused.

Sullivan didn't speak.

"And then there's a smiley face," Active went on. "And then this: 'makes me wonder what you had on underneath,' followed by three question marks."

Sullivan's face turned a mottled red and he looked like a little boy caught stealing candy.

"Does that jog your memory? I can go on. There's lots more."

"I didn't mean any harm, it was just words," Sullivan stammered. "You know, something to break the monotony up there. I'm not even sure she got them. She never responded."

"Is that why you went to Chukchi? To get a response?"

"No." Sullivan's fists were balled up on his knees.

"Maybe you figured when you were both away from the job, things might be different, might get a little more personal?"

"No!" Sullivan was almost shouting now. "I'm a married man."

"The thing is, Fred, you were in Chukchi around the time

141

we believe Shalene was killed."

"So what?"

"So there's a picture coming together here is what. You send her sexually explicit e-mails, she's not interested. But you can't leave it at that, you show up in Chukchi and she turns up dead. You can see how that looks, right?"

"You're twisting things around. I didn't send her anymore e-mails after the middle of May." He pointed at a Dell laptop on an end table. "They're all on there, see for yourself. I realized it was a stupid thing to do."

"Because you knew she was dead?"

"What?" His face deepened to red-purple and he slapped the table so hard Active's pen bounced onto the rug. "I didn't know she was dead until you came to my office and told me. You've got it all wrong."

Active retrieved his pen and made a show of finding the right page in his notebook. "Then this would be the time to tell me exactly what you did in Chukchi."

Chiquita resumed her frantic yipping from the bathroom.

"Damn dog!" Sullivan shouted. "Chiquita! Shut the fuck up!"

The yipping got louder and higher. Sullivan wiped his forehead. "All right, all right. You have to understand, I didn't go to Chukchi to see Shalene. I knew she had flown down there the day before, and once I arrived, yes, I was thinking about her. I stopped by the market to kill time and I just kept thinking, hell, why not go see her. It was nothing but a stupid impulse, okay? It sounds ridiculous now, but I thought I'd drop by, we could talk, see how we got along, see if there was a chance."

"A chance for what?"

"Shalene was a really nice girl. I thought we might get closer. Look, I know it sounds bad. But I'm not one of those dirty old men, I'm not like that. I'm - -"

"A married man?"

Sullivan bit his lip with a cornered look.

"Did you do more than think about meeting Shalene?"

"Yeah, okay, I knew she stayed with Kim Tulimaq. I took a taxi. The driver knew the house, small town, you know. I thought I'd bring some doughnuts to brighten up her morning, say I happened to be in town, which was true, and we'd take it from there. I guess it wasn't much of a plan."

"You went to Kim's house?"

"Yes. I knocked several times, but there was nobody home."

"What time was this?"

"I don't remember exactly. It was still morning but not real early. Nine, ten, maybe?"

"How do you know no one was home? Maybe they were asleep. Was Kim's four-wheeler parked out front?"

Sullivan paused for a moment, worked his tongue against the inside of his cheek. "No, there was a snowmachine under a cover by the house but no four-wheeler."

"Could it have been around back?"

"No, it wasn't, I checked there, too."

"Really?"

"Just a walk-around to see it there were any signs of life."

"And maybe look in the windows, too?"

"Well, a quick look, but I didn't see anything. It was dark in there."

"And then what did you do?"

"I kind of, well …"

"You were going to tell me exactly what you did in Chukchi."

"Okay. I got a little nosy."

"Nosy how?"

"I took Chiquita with me and knocked on the door to the arctic entry again. I waited a couple minutes but no one answered. I tried knocking harder and the door pushed open a little. Then the inner door did, too, like it wasn't shut tight and the pressure from the outer door made it give. It just happened. I didn't break in."

"Of course not. What did you do then?"

"I took a little peek inside. All the lights were out. It was real quiet, still. I was holding Chiquita and she never let out a peep. If there was anybody in there, she would have raised a ruckus, for sure. So I backed out the door feeling like the biggest fool that ever lived, thinking why didn't I call and scope out the situation before going over there? I called the cab again and went back to the airport and stayed there till my flight boarded for Anchorage."

"You left for Anchorage without seeing Shalene or Kim?"

"Right."

"Did you leave them the doughnuts?"

"There was a trash bin set out by the road. It must have been trash pickup day. I tossed them in there."

Active pictured the city's new plastic rollout bins with the supposedly animal-proof latching tops. They worked about as well as the old ones, because nothing was animal-proof in Chukchi.

"Too bad. Nobody got to enjoy them except maybe the

ravens."

Sullivan grunted and shrugged.

Active turned to a new page of his notebook, then looked up, pen in mid-air. "Let me make sure I have it straight. This was the day after Shalene left the Slope?"

"Yes."

"So the sixteenth. May sixteenth."

"Yes."

"Did you try to contact her after that?"

"I called her from the airport that night when I was leaving Chukchi."

"And?"

"The call went to voicemail."

"And your phone records would verify that?"

"Yes."

"I'll have to take your laptop as evidence, so we can verify what you said about the e-mails."

Sullivan paused, picked up the computer, held it in mid-air for a moment, then handed it to Active. "Take it, but I don't see what a few of my e-mails have to do with a murder investigation."

"Unwelcome advances often play a part in this kind of crime when the victim is a young woman."

"Advances?" Sullivan's face reddened again. He leaned forward as if to jump to his feet, then he sagged back into his chair. "Well, I wouldn't exactly call it advan - - anyway, it's more likely this is some random act of violence, right? There's a lot of drinking and drugs in those Bush villages. Maybe Shalene just happened to cross paths with the wrong person at the wrong time, one of the locals."

Active tapped his pen against the notebook. "Well, I have to tell you, Fred, this doesn't look like a crime of chance. It looks personal. We think Shalene knew her killer."

"You're not saying it was someone at North Slope Environmental?"

"It's possible."

"I hope you don't seriously think that I - - nobody kills anyone over some stupid e-mails, right?" He forced out a nervous laugh. "Probably some young hothead, that's who you should be looking for."

"Anyone in particular?"

"No, I mean I'm not accusing anyone. But ..."

"But what?"

"I'm not saying he did anything to Shalene."

"Who?"

"Josh McCarran. Before that fight with Larry Hayden, he had a couple of previous altercations over women."

"What kind of altercations?"

"Some cursing, shoving, there might have been a punch or two thrown. A little territory-marking over a new female on the job, from what I remember. Boys being boys."

"There was nothing like that in his file."

"That was before we had the crackdown on...workplace violence is what OSHA calls it. My way of dealing with it was to give them a good talking-to, keep it out of the official record. But by the time Hayden and McCarran got into it, the big bosses had their shorts in a twist, didn't want the feds coming down on us, and we were totally into this zero-tolerance bullshit. So I had to write the two of them up."

"Why did you decide to mention this now?"

"For Shalene, of course. Whatever I can do to help."

Yeah, Active thought, help yourself.

"Right," he said.

On his way to the airport, he punched up the number for Pat Carnaby, head of the Alaska State Trooper detachment in Chukchi. Carnaby had been one of Active's instructors at the Trooper academy in Sitka, then his boss after they both ended up in Chukchi, back in the days before Active got the chief's job at Public Safety. Carnaby had been around so long, had worked in so many different places, he knew everybody worth knowing in Alaska law enforcement.

He was breathing heavily when he answered the phone.

"Pat? You all right?"

"Nathan. Whew. Yeah, I'm at the rec center. Trying to get the gut under control, but right now I feel like the gut's winning." Carnaby's laugh turned into a coughing fit. "Hold on," he wheezed.

The cough subsided and Active heard water being chugged.

"Ok. Better. What's up?"

"We've got this murder case you might be able to help with."

"Shalene Harvey, I'm guessing? Found in pieces in Tent City?"

"That's the one."

"Sure, whatever you need."

"Do you still have that source in juvenile records in Anchorage?"

"Oh, please. Who am I checking on?"

"Guy named Joshua McCarran, assault from eight or nine years ago. Female victim."

"I'll make a call. Is this guy your suspect?"

"One of three."

"Feast or famine, right? I don't know which is worse."

"Tell me about it."

CHAPTER FIFTEEN

· August 31 ·

CHUKCHI

"Nothing on Twitter or Instagram, but look at her Facebook page." Lucy scrolled the screen of her office computer through Kim Tulimaq's posts.

Active pulled a chair up beside her and dropped into it for a closer look. "Lots of fishing and hunting photos," he said.

"She's a real Chukchi girl, all right." Lucy stopped at a photo of Tulimaq on one knee, in front of a turquoise plywood cabin on the tundra, smiling over a field-dressed caribou. An Alaska flag unfurled above the cabin door. The caption read: "Got this big one up the Katonak—stew tonight, *aarigaa!*"

"What about likes and comments?" Active asked. "Any anti-gay stuff, threats, that kind of thing?"

"It's a private page," Lucy said. "She's got it set up so only her friends can see it."

Lucy clicked on the thumbs-up symbol under the caribou photo. A long list of names popped up. "Seem like maybe they're all like her, from the ones I recognize. The comments since they heard about Shalene being killed are just condolences, sorry for your loss, that kind of thing."

"So you're friends with Kim on Facebook? How well do you know her?"

"Barely at all," Lucy said. "And we're not Facebook friends. I'm just using my Aunt Jennie's log-on. She's like Kim and Shalene, all right."

"You mean - -"

"Ah-hah."

"Huh. Has she heard any scuttlebutt in that community about who killed Shalene?"

"No. She just told me they're all scared it might be somebody trying to kill people like them."

"Well, you can tell her we don't think so."

"I already did," Lucy said. "Anyway, she follows my page, so I asked her about using her log-on."

"That would be your Tundra Treats page?"

Lucy was famous around Chukchi for the Inupiat recipes she collected and posted on Facebook. Even Active's mother, Martha Johnson, had commented to him about the recipe for duck soup she had found on the page. He suspected a good many of Lucy's recipes went up during work hours, but he had resisted the temptation to check the time stamps on her posts and find out. She got her work done, which was what mattered. Another case, he had concluded, where wisdom lay in knowing what not to notice.

Lucy shot him a sideways glance, no doubt wondering if she was being busted.

Active grinned. "Which of course is great community relations for our department."

Lucy relaxed.

"Those posts are from last fall," he said. "What about the

more recent ones?"

"Those ones are different." Lucy scrolled up so quickly that most of the photos blurred by before Active could process what he was seeing.

She stopped on a photo of Tulimaq in full lip-lock with a young woman with golden–brown hair. Active leaned in closer, and, yes, she was definitely Shalene Harvey.

Lucy scrolled up more slowly. "They're not shy about it, ah?"

"Definitely not." Kim and Shalene smooched with their heads propped on pillows against a headboard in what looked like Kim's bedroom. They hugged cheek-to-cheek, mouths puckered in smooch mode. In one dim, grainy video they appeared to be engaged in foreplay until Kim picked up the phone, grinned into it, and stopped the recording.

"Are there more like that?" Active shook his head in disbelief at the blurry line between what people considered public and private.

"Sorry to disappoint you," Lucy said. "That's the only 'R' rated one I found."

Now her screen showed the lovers huddled next to each other on the edge of a bed. Both wore stocking caps, night shirts, and knee-high socks. They grinned and held their left hands out to the camera to display matching rings.

Lucy read the caption: "Promised to each other, so in love. K + S 4 ever," Lucy read.

"Forever, huh?"

"Every girl wants the happily ever after." She shot him another side-eye and, he thought, paused to see if he would respond.

And suddenly they were not two people trying to solve a murder, but ex-lovers on the brink of falling into the same old swamp of might've-beens. The past is never dead, somebody smart had once said, or really even past.

Neither were relationships, as far as Active was concerned.

"Nice scrollwork on the rings," he said, now giving Lucy a side-eye of his own. Would she let it go?

She leaned in and studied the rings. He relaxed.

"That post was in March," she said.

Active recognized the scrollwork. He'd seen it on Tulimaq's ring during their first interview and on the ring they'd found in Tent City. "Lovers forever in March and two months later, Shalene's dead."

Active's cell rang and Pat Carnaby's ID came up. He stood to take the call in his office and said, "Hang on a sec, Pat."

"Good work," he told Lucy. "Can you print out all the posts from January forward in chronological order?"

She looked into his eyes and he realized he'd put a hand on her shoulder without thinking about it. He pulled it away.

"From January all the way until now?" she asked

"Yes, please. Okay?"

"*Arii,* that'll take too long."

"Hey, you're getting paid to hang out on Facebook, right?"

She rolled her eyes, rattled her keyboard a few seconds, and the printer whirred to life.

Active closed the door to his office and got back to his call. "Pat, I didn't expect to hear from you so soon."

"My source got right back to me," Carnaby said. "Must have been a slow day at the office."

"And?"

"Josh McCarran was arrested for assault when he was

seventeen. He threatened a sixteen-year-old girl with a knife. Apparently they were dating at the time."

"Huh. Was she injured?"

"Not by the knife. Some bruises and scratches."

"And he skated?"

"More or less. He was charged, but the charges were dropped almost immediately. The usual story—well known old-Alaska family with money, the grandfather was a famous guide, they had this kickass Seattle lawyer named Fortune. Plus, the girlfriend wasn't cooperative and there were no priors on McCarran, so the DA apparently decided it wasn't worth the paperwork."

"No priors or they just weren't reported?"

"Always a possibility. Like they say, justice is blind, especially if you're connected."

Carnaby paused, took a deep breath. "So you heard about Bachner, right?"

"From the Academy? What - -"

"Well, he, ah, he went out on his dock with his Glock and a flask of Jack, and he shot at the ducks on the lake till he finished the flask, then he, ah, well, he ate the Glock."

Active could think of nothing to say, so he didn't.

"Nathan?"

"What a break for the ducks."

"Same old smartass, huh?" Carnaby was silent for a while. "You're talking to somebody about this, right?"

"You too?" Active said under his breath, then to Carnaby, "Don't worry, I'm handling it. It's not a big deal."

"Not a big deal. You got any idea how much trouble you're in here, Nathan?"

"Thanks for the info on McCarran." Active tapped off before Carnaby could say anything else.

He stared at his cell until the screen dimmed. Then he pulled his Glock from the holster on his belt, laid it on the blotter.

He sat down, stared at the gun, picked it up, extracted the clip and laid it on the blotter.

He palmed the weapon, now just a gray hunk of polymer and steel, but somehow heavier than it should be. He had to use both hands to lift it to chin height, turn it around, and tilt the muzzle toward his mouth. He shuddered and pointed it away again.

But how *would* a Glock taste? Had Bachner thought about it for a while, or had he just done it?

Active's hands were shaking now. He lowered the gun back to the blotter, laid his palms flat, and closed his eyes.

When he opened them a few seconds later, Grace was at the window of his office door, her face a study in bewilderment and terror. He had forgotten they were meeting for an early lunch.

Active pulled open his right-hand file drawer and dropped in the gun and clip.

Grace was inside now, still with that look on her face. He tried a smile. It felt more like a grimace.

"Hey, sweetie," he said. His voice cracked.

She walked around the desk as he rose, and stood toe to toe with him, looking up into his eyes. Her lower lip trembled. "What was that?"

"Nothing. I was unloading it, putting it away."

"No, baby, no." She put her hands on his upper arms and stroked them. "That was not nothing. I saw your face."

He shook his head. Panic knotted his stomach, squeezed his lungs, made his heart race, threatened to explode in his head. He couldn't let this happen in front of her. He willed himself to breathe slow and shallow.

She searched his face, then the quicksilver eyes flashed. "Nathan Active, I know what you were thinking with that gun in your hand. But you're not going to leave me and Nita and Charlie like that. I won't let you. You have to stop shutting me out. You have to talk to me."

He wrapped her in his arms, held her against his chest, more for his own comfort than hers.

"Not now, sweetie. I just can't right now." He squeezed her tighter. "I'll handle it." Wetness seeped through his shirt where she pressed her cheek.

Why couldn't he talk to her, he wondered as held her and breathed in her lavender scent. It was like he was playing himself these days, performing an impression of the man he had been before the shooting on the bridge.

She pulled back, swiping under her eyes with the heels of her hands. "I know you think you have to be this big, strong bullet-proof cop who's not afraid of anything. But you're human. It's okay to need help."

He nodded, more in avoidance than agreement. "I'll handle it," he said again.

He lifted her chin and kissed her.

"I'm sorry, I should have called before you came down here," he said. "But I have to go. Something's come up on the case."

He took his cell and keys from the desk and brushed past her to retrieve his jacket from its hook on the wall.

She followed him toward the door. "What about your gun?"

He opened the door for her. "I don't need it."

"Am I supposed to trust that you know what you're doing?"

"Yes."

They went downstairs to the parking lot and he held her again beside her Jeep SUV.

"I'll see you tonight," he said.

"Really?" Her voice was husky in his ear.

"Really." He squeezed her, hard. "Really. Give Charlie a kiss for me, ah?"

He climbed into his Tahoe, drove to the seawall, and parked beside Chukchi Bay. He shut down the engine, switched off Kay-Chuck on the radio, leaned against the headrest, and studied the thin ribbon of light that separated gray sky from gray water.

When he stirred and checked his cell phone, it showed he had somehow been there nearly a half hour. His heartbeat and breathing were normal again. He stared into the rearview mirror.

"Don't worry," he told his reflection. "I'm handling it."

CHAPTER SIXTEEN

·August 31 ·

CHUKCHI

He started the Tahoe, drove around the west end of the airport, and headed down the Loop Road toward Tent City. Nothing new had really come up on the case, despite what he had told Grace.

But the same old collection of loose ends always bouncing around in his head were telling him to take another walk through the Atoyuk camp where Tommie had spent her childhood summers.

Maybe something would jump out at him. Long immersion in a case, he had learned, tended to sensitize the faculties. Something you'd missed before would seem so obvious on the second pass—or the tenth—that it was like a switch had been thrown.

And he could combine the walk-through with some practice with the AR-15 mounted on the Tahoe's console. With the Glock locked away in his desk, the AR-15 was his compromise with the realities of police work and his need to push the Bachner story out of his head.

He would collect a couple dozen cans and bottles from the littered beach in front of Tent City, toss them into the

157

Chukchi Sea, and sink them as they bobbed on the surf. Chukchi didn't have a shooting range to maintain firearms proficiency, so the beach and the city dump were long established as the semi-official stand-ins.

It still didn't land quite right with Active—shooting at bottles on the water instead of paper bull's-eyes on a cable and pulley. But it was pure Chukchi, he had to give it that, the cop version of the "LET 'EM" motto.

At the north end of Tent City, he turned right off the Loop Road and threaded the Tahoe through the alders and tundra to the beach. He parked beside the narrow gravel track that ran along the bluff separating the beach from the brush, shacks, and tent frames of the camping area.

He released the AR from its mount on the console, climbed out, slung the weapon across his back, and started down the path.

To his right and a few feet below, a ten-yard belt of gravel beach met slate-colored waves rolling in on the stiff west wind. The day was a warning shot from winter, with pellet snow pecking on his duty jacket and stinging his cheeks as he made his way along the bluff.

Up ahead a triangular blue-and-yellow flag flapped from a spruce pole that had been shoved into dirt on the edge of the bluff. Thirty yards farther on, the orange-yellow flames of a campfire danced in the wind.

And a few feet from the fire, arms and legs flailed and heads bobbed over a writhing figure who was screaming "*Arii,* let me up!"

Active raced back to the Tahoe and locked the AR-15 inside—no way he wanted a firearm on his person if he was in for a wrestling match—and rushed down the slope and across the gravel.

It was three teenagers on one, he saw as he came up to the fight. One big guy holding a little one down while two others pummeled him.

"Hey!" he yelled. "Police! Knock it off!"

He waded in and pulled them apart. The big guy stood up and crossed his arms with a smirk. The little guy curled into a fetal position and put his arms over his face.

"You three!" he said in his command voice. "Get back by the fire. Sit down and empty your pockets. IDs and everything else."

The attackers complied, tossing cigarette packs, keys, loose change, driver's licenses, and a couple of joints into a heap on the sand. Active knelt over the victim and uncovered his face. He didn't seem to be marked up.

"We're just goofing around," the big guy said with a grin. He was way past two hundred pounds, but not more than five-six in height. "We were doing an action scene, like in the movies with a stunt man, no real hitting. Tell him, Isaac."

Isaac brushed dirt from his face and hair and sat up. "Yeah, we were p-p-p-playing." He squeezed his eyes shut and sprayed out spit as he struggled to speak. "I'm o-kuh-kuh-kay."

Active scooped up the IDs from the pile on the gravel and studied them, then turned to the big guy. "You're Eugene, right? Eugene Wilson."

"They call me Big."

"Big what?"

"Just Big."

"All right, Big, let me guess. When you do your stunt fights, Isaac here always gets to play the punching bag."

"Yeah." Big grinned again. "He yells pretty good, like we're really hitting him."

One of the other stunt men, who wore a knit cap and denim jacket and had pink headphones with big cups around his neck, scooted closer to the fire, picked up an open beer, and took a long gulp. He was Kenny Goodwin, according to his ID.

The fourth player, a skinny kid in a camo hoodie whose driver's license said he was Moses Atuk, moved next to Kenny.

Isaac inched closer to the fire but hunched and hugged his knees, making himself smaller. Big lowered his bulk onto a log across from the others.

Active drew his notebook and pen from his pocket, took down their names, then returned the IDs. "You guys come down here a lot?"

"Sometimes," Big said. "This is our spot. We marked it with that flag, ah?" He pointed up at the bluff. "We always make a fire here. Nobody bothers us."

"Nobody ever comes by to hang out, bum a smoke, have a beer?"

"Nah," Big said. "We never saw anybody the whole time we been coming here."

"That right? Tent City is right up over the bluff. You never saw anybody come down from there?"

Big stroked his chin as if giving the question serious thought. "No one except ..."

"Except?"

"Except you, Five-Oh." He laughed. "Ah, guys?"

Kenny and Moses echoed Big's laugh and nodded. Isaac looked confused for a moment, then nodded, too, with a smile that looked forced.

Active moved to where Big sat, stood over him, caught his eyes, and gave him the cop look. "You watch too much

TV, ah, Big?"

Big broke the gaze and dropped his eyes.

Active squatted down to eye level with the crew. According to their IDs they were all either eighteen or nineteen. Too young to be drinking, and it looked like they might be making a day of it as it was only a little past noon. But he decided not to sweat them about the beer or the joints, not yet. He wanted to keep them talking. His radar told him Big was lying about never seeing anyone else around. The place was out of the way, but not truly secluded.

"What do you guys do when you're not out here?" Active asked.

"I work at the E-Z Market," Big said. "Moses is gonna start there next week."

"How about you, Kenny?"

Kenny, the one with the pink headphones, chucked his empty into the fire, poked it with a stick, and watched the aluminum blacken and warp. He shrugged. "I fish with my uncle sometimes." He pulled up his jacket collar so it partly concealed the headphones.

The headphone cups, Active saw, bore a stylized "b" logo. They weren't the cheap, generic kind but a brand he'd seen on sports stars in commercials. Just not in that bright shade of pink. His radar was pinging again.

"That's some nice headphones you got there, Kenny."

"Yeah, they're Beats, man."

"Expensive, ah?"

Kenny shrugged again.

"But pink. You take those from a girl, maybe, your sister or something?"

"What? Nah, I found 'em." He worried his toe into the beach gravel and kicked some of it at the fire. "Somebody threw 'em away and I found 'em."

"Somebody threw away a set of Beats? Where did you find them?"

"On the beach."

Big grunted and spat into the fire.

Kenny shot him a wary glance.

"Where exactly on the beach?"

Big spat again.

"I don't remember," Kenny mumbled. "Somewhere around here, I guess. It was a long time ago."

"Around here, but on the beach, not somewhere else?"

"Like where?" Kenny asked, kicking at the gravel again.

"Like Tent City?"

"Nah, we don't go up there except when Big's auntie's there during fishing season."

Isaac pulled his chin lower into his jacket and twisted one hand inside the other.

Kenny's story sounded as sketchy as Big's claim they had never seen anyone else around their hangout site.

"Can I see them?" Active asked. "I'm thinking about getting some for my daughter."

Kenny glanced at Big again, unwrapped the headphones from his neck, and handed them over.

Active tried them on, then took them off and ran his fingers along the edge of the headband. The surface was rippled and darkened. "What happened here?" Active asked. "They get too close to a fire?"

"Don't know," Kenny said. "They were like that when I found 'em.".

Active turned the headphones in his hand, looked at the inside of the headband. A set of initials were lettered there in white nail polish: **SH**.

Active glanced up at the bluff. The old Atoyuk place, where Shalene Harvey had ended up, was just over the rise and a few yards back.

"Who did you say threw these away?"

Kenny looked at the fire. "I didn't see. I just found 'em."

"I'm going to need to take these with me," Active said.

Kenny jerked his head around and bent his knee like he was about to stand up. "What? Why? You can't … I didn't steal them. Right, guys?" He glanced around at the others. "You saw me find 'em, ah?"

Moses poked at the fire with a stick. Isaac threw Active a frightened look, then cast his eyes down again. Big sat still, tight-lipped. Apparently none of them wanted to risk defending Kenny's property rights to illegal alcohol exactly like what was in their possession.

Active held up the headphones and looked at the initials again. "These may be evidence in a murder case."

Isaac's head jerked up. "M-m-murder? You mean they belonged to the k-k-killer?"

"Or the victim," Active said. "Either way, they're coming with me, and we're going to have to search this area for other evidence."

"Let 'em." Kenny shrugged. "Easy come, easy go."

"Put out that fire, and gather up your stuff," Active said. "Your hangout spot is now off limits. Except the beer. Leave that where it is. You're all underage and you're lucky I don't arrest you."

Big guzzled the rest of his beer, crumpled the can in half, and lobbed it into the fire. The rest threw their cans into the fire, beer and all. They kicked sand onto the fire until just embers and a few dying flames were left.

"Where we gonna go?" Moses asked.

"Let's hang out at my auntie's tent in Tent City," Big said. "She's probably there all week and she cooks."

Kenny leaned over to retrieve the items from their emptied pockets. Moses picked up a Styrofoam ice chest.

Isaac grabbed a backpack and stepped back from the others. "I-I- g--gotta go home," he said.

"What the fuck, man?" Big said. "You not gonna walk all that way. Come with us."

"Nah. I g-gotta help my dad with his tr-tr-truck."

"Whatever, man," Big said. "C'mon, guys." He looked back at Isaac as the others walked toward the bluff.

When the three others were out of earshot, Active asked Isaac, "Where do you live?"

"Second Street by the church."

"I'll give you a ride. I'm parked at the end of Tent City, that way." He pointed north.

Isaac looked up the beach to where his buddies were climbing the bluff. Big looked back in Isaac's direction again.

"C-c-can you go ahead, and I'll meet you there in a few minutes?"

Active followed Isaac's eyes up to the figures disappearing over the bluff. Isaac didn't want to be seen having an extended chat with the police, which was a good sign, Active thought.

He waited fifteen minutes in the Tahoe. The sky had darkened and hung low over the sea. The wind had picked up. It looked like Isaac wasn't going to show. He started the engine and was about to pull away when Isaac materialized at the passenger door and hauled his thin frame up into the seat. He was breathing hard, as if he had run a good part of the way.

Active inched the Tahoe around and started back along

the bluff path toward the point where he could cut over to the Loop Road and head back to town. Isaac didn't speak, just stared straight ahead, silent.

"Your buddies said they have jobs," Active said as they bounced along. "How about you?"

"Nah," Isaac said. He opened his mouth and closed it again as if he wanted to say more but didn't know where to start.

"You got something going on this summer besides hanging out with your crew?"

Isaac turned to look at Active and almost smiled. "I'm leaving for UAF next week."

"So you graduated from high school this year?"

"Yeah."

"What're you gonna study over there in Fairbanks?"

Isaac drew his chin into his chest and looked up at Active as they pulled out onto the smoother surface of the Loop Road. "W-w-water and environmental s-s-s-science."

"Great. Good luck."

Isaac nodded and met Active's eyes with a crooked smile before turning to stare out the windshield again. Active let the silence hang between them. He could hear Isaac's hands fiddling with his backpack on the floor between his legs.

"W-we were down on the beach after g-g-graduation," Isaac sputtered out.

Active's radar pinged again. High school graduation. That had been in May. Mid-May.

"Yeah? Just you, Big, Kenny, and Moses?"

"Yeah, at first." Isaac kept his eyes straight ahead.

"And then someone else showed up?"

"Yeah. This guy. It was weird. His hands were all bloody."

Isaac's breath was coming hard again.

"Take your time, Isaac. Tell me about this guy with the bloody hands."

"He came down the beach toward us, but it was like he didn't even see us. He just stare with fire in his eyes like he's really pissed off and he almost walked right into us."

"Did you recognize him?"

"Nah, he wasn't from Chukchi. He was a *naluaqmiu* with a big bushy beard."

"A bushy beard?"

"Yep. A big, bushy, black beard."

"Can you describe him other than the beard? Height, weight, age?" Active wanted to pull over and get out his notebook, but he was afraid Isaac would stop talking.

"He was t-t-tall, like six feet maybe."

"And his weight? Age?" Active prodded.

"Two hundred, maybe, big, but not really fat." Isaac said. "Older than us, but not that much. Hard to tell with a *naluaqmiu*. They all kinda look alike."

"So he walked toward you?" Active asked.

"Yeah," Isaac said. "He came up to us. He was weird, all right. He had two backpacks."

"Two?"

"Yeah, a regular one on his back and he was holding another one in front." Isaac crossed his arms over his chest. "It was a little leather one, like a girl's. The way he was holding it, that's when I saw his knuckles were all bloody."

Active edged the Tahoe toward the side of the road. They were past the airport now and at the south end of Second Street, not far from Isaac's house near the church. "I'm going to pull over, so I can listen better, okay?"

Isaac nodded. Active parked and turned off the engine.

He took out his notebook and pen and simultaneously asked the next question before Isaac could object to having his words taken down.

"Was one hand bloody or both?"

"Both." Isaac took a breath. "Big said, 'Hey, man, you hurt?' The guy just looked at him like he didn't understand. Big said, 'Your hands are bleeding, man,' and he looked down at them like he didn't even know anything was wrong. Big asked him, 'You been in a fight?' He said, 'No.'"

The words were spilling out of Isaac now.

"Then Kenny said, 'What's in that girlie pack, man?' He didn't say anything. He just held it tighter and stared. So Kenny said, he said, 'Let's see what's in it.' The guy just stared, so Kenny grabbed it and Big and them took a look. The guy didn't do anything, like he's scared." Isaac chuckled. "Like he's trying not to get his ass beat by some Native kids."

"What was in the pack?"

"Some girl's stuff, makeup, a girl's wallet. A knife."

"What kind of knife?"

"Like a hunting knife in a leather sheath. And some headphones. Beats headphones."

"Kenny's headphones?"

"Yeah, but he didn't steal 'em, like he said. The guy threw 'em away, all right."

"The man with the beard?"

"Yeah." Isaac's voice was rising, his words quickening.

"Big opened the wallet and the guy just grabbed it out of his hand, grabbed everything, the headphones, the knife, the other stuff, the pack and threw it all on the fire. Then he said, 'I've got to go.' Big said, 'Where you going, man? You don't like our company? You should have a beer with us.' And the guy said, 'No thanks,' like that." Isaac did his best to mimic a low, deliberate voice. "'No thanks. I have to go to the airport.' Then he walked off."

"And Kenny pulled the headphones out of the fire?"

"Yep. They were Beats."

Active scribbled rapidly in his notebook to get it all down. "What about the rest of the stuff, the knife?"

"We let it burn."

"Even the wallet?"

"Yeah. Big said wasn't no money in it. Just a driver's license."

"Did you see whose driver's license?" Active asked.

"I just saw it quick before the guy grabbed it. Big held it up to us, said, 'Ooh, look at her. She's hot.' It was a pretty girl in the picture, but not a local."

"How do you know she wasn't a local girl?"

"I saw the address. It was Nome." Isaac looked down and took a deep breath like he was relieved to have all those words out. "That's why I told you about it."

"What?"

"Because of that girl. And the blood on his hands. I thought maybe he did something to that girl."

"You did the right thing."

Isaac smiled his crooked smile again.

"Now, you said this was right after graduation?" Active asked.

"Yeah, two days after."

"And that was?"

"The middle of May, I forget the date."

Active started the Tahoe and eased back onto Second Street. "Thanks for talking to me. Let's get you home."

"Uh, c-could you let me off before you get all the way there? If my dad sees me get out of a police car, he might think I'm in t-trouble."

"No problem."

Isaac fidgeted with his backpack again. "The guys aren't in trouble, are they?"

"No, just bad liars."

"Y-y-you won't tell them I talked to you?"

"No need."

Active dropped Isaac off near St. Mark's, then punched Kavik's contact on his cell. The AR-15 practice would have to wait.

"What's up, Chief?" Kavik answered.

"Meet me on the beach at the north end of Tent City with some police tape and a shovel. And come to think of it, a fire extinguisher."

"What's on fire?"

"Josh McCarran's story." Active stayed on his cell and filled Kavik in with the information from Isaac while he sped back to the beach.

They reached the campfire site at about the same time, Kavik with a shovel and fire extinguisher, Active with his own folding shovel from the back of the Tahoe.

Kavik sprayed foam on the smoldering fire and remnants of scorched beer cans.

"It looks like this fire pit gets pretty heavy use," he said. "Do we really expect to find anything from Shalene's backpack after three months?"

"Let's see."

They pulled on gloves and took turns, scraping, shoveling, and swiping away the ash and debris layer by layer. Within a few minutes they had amassed a pile of broken bottles, mangled cans, charred foil from food wrappers, the blackened rubber sole of a Sorel boot, and a bicycle chain.

"Doesn't look like much of anything," Kavik said. "Should we go down deeper?"

"No. Tape off this area to a ten-foot perimeter and get a team out here to do a wider search."

Active planted the shovel at the edge of the pit to free his hands so he could remove his gloves. The spade clanked against metal. He knelt and brushed a gloved hand over the blackened ground. His middle finger caught on the tip of something hard and sharp. He drew his belt knife and scraped ash away from the sides of the object,

"What have you got there?" Kavik asked.

Active picked up the item between two fingers, tapped away the ash with his other hand, and held it up for inspection.

"Whoa," Kavik said.

"Looks like a nine-inch, non-serrated knife to me."

"Our murder weapon?"

"Could be. The handle's burnt to hell, but the blade is intact. Express it down to Georgeanne on the afternoon jet and see if you can sweet-talk her into a first-impression readout sometime tomorrow, okay?

"Roger," Kavik said.

"And I want you to oversee the search of the area personally."

"Right. And what's your next move?"

"Getting back to the Slope as fast as possible." Active waved the knife. "It's time for another run at Josh McCarran."

CHAPTER SEVENTEEN

· September 1 ·

DEADHORSE, PRUDHOE BAY

"As fast as possible" turned out to mean an afternoon trip to Anchorage, a night in a heroically misnamed fleabag called the Paradise Inn, then a mid-morning flight that put him in Deadhorse just before noon.

McCarran scowled in surprise as Active dropped into a chair across from him in the North Slope Environmental cafeteria. "What now? You trying to get me fired?"

"Oh, just a few follow-up questions," Active said. He drew out his notebook and pen as slowly as possible to let McCarran stew.

McCarran forked up a bite of meatloaf, looked at it, and set it back on his plate amid the din of Slopers at lunch around them. He pulled at his beard.

"You know, Josh, sometimes investigating a case means being a part-time psychologist."

"So this is therapy?"

"I observe behavior. I look at patterns. For example, the way you're pulling at your beard. That's a pattern."

McCarran looked at his hand and laid it on the table. "So? What's the big deal? Are you going to write in your notebook that I pulled my beard?"

Active smiled. "It's not a big deal, which is the point. You've done it so often, it's automatic. If you shave your beard off today, for the next few days you'll keep reaching for it even though it's gone."

"What's the point? I have to get back to work."

"From what I hear, whenever you get competition for a woman, you come out swinging. Asserting yourself as the alpha male, that's another pattern for you."

"I guess. That's nature, right?"

"The biggest bull moose gets the cow?"

"Yeah."

"So what if the other moose is a cow, not a bull? Does that mess things up?"

"Yeah, well, I don't brawl with women if that's what you're saying."

"Right. That throws the pattern out of whack. This time, you're in competition with Kim for Shalene, so you retreat, is that right?"

McCarran frowned with a thoughtful look. Behind the food service counter, dishes rattled and clanked in the kitchen. A country song played feebly from a speaker in the center of the ceiling. After a moment, Active remembered the title from hearing it several times a day on Kay-Chuck: "Keep Your Hands to Yourself." He grinned as he waited for McCarran to come up with an answer.

"I didn't want any more trouble," McCarran said finally. "Shay wanted to be done, so I backed off. Like I told you before."

"Right. That's what bothers me. It's uncharacteristic. You can't break a pattern that easily. What I think is, you backed off because you saw a way to still have what you wanted."

"Yeah? How was I going to do that? Go up to Kim's, break down her door, grab Shay, and take off on the four-wheeler? If that happened, Kim would have already told you. Or is this all coming from her?"

"Maybe you are telling the truth about going to Kim's house. But instead of banging on the door, you waited outside until Shalene came out. Somehow you hooked up with her."

A man in a stained apron swished a mop back and forth over the cafeteria floor near the entrance. A bearded man in a baseball cap ducked his head into the door, scanned the room, then ducked back out.

"That's a great story, but that's all it is, a story. Didn't happen. When I left Kim's, I walked around a while and then went to the airport like I said. Alone."

"Whatever happened, you didn't go directly to the airport, did you?"

McCarran hesitated. "I said I walked around for a while. So?"

"Were you planning to get rid of her backpack with all her other stuff after you killed her?"

"How do you know about the back - -? There was no plan. I grabbed it off the trailer on Kim's four-wheeler. It was with Shay's other stuff, her jacket, a couple suitcases, outside Kim's door."

"That doesn't make sense, does it, Josh? She had texted you she was staying with Kim. Why would she have all her belongings in the four-wheeler trailer like she was leaving?"

McCarran shrugged. "She must have been almost ready to come meet me when Kim got in her head and changed her mind. But, I didn't see her. I didn't kill her."

"The evidence says different."

"What evidence?"

"We've recovered the knife that was in Shalene's backpack, the backpack last seen in your possession."

Active held up his phone with a photo of the knife from the campfire pit on the screen.

"This knife, Josh. We think it's the murder weapon. We found it near where we found her body."

"Murder weapon? I didn't even know there was a knife in the pack."

"Sure you did. We have witnesses."

McCarran's eyes bounced from side to side like he was trying to figure out how he had slipped up. "Those kids. Dammit!" He slammed a fist on the table. "They tried to steal the pack. They dumped it out. That's the only time I saw the knife."

Active let it ride, watching.

"They could have killed her," McCarran went on. "You should look into that. They were high. They looked violent."

"How did you injure your hands? Was that from beating her up? Or maybe you cut yourself while you were carving her up?"

McCarran shuddered and looked at his hands as though the blood from that day was still there. "I busted my knuckles banging on Kim's door. I don't know anything about a body. I was at the airport."

"Patterns, Josh. Lying. That's another one of your patterns."

"Okay, I'll come clean. I took the backpack off the four-wheeler at Kim's, that's the truth. I knew Shay kept her important stuff in that pack, her wallet, her headphones. But, I didn't look inside. I didn't know about the knife. I only took it so she couldn't have her stuff. I wanted to hurt her because I was pissed."

"So you admit to theft. You're not exactly making yourself look good here."

"I wasn't thinking straight. I told you I was pissed."

"Your male ego took a hit, and you made a bad decision. That happen a lot with Shalene?"

"Yeah, she could get me twisted like that. If I never went to Kim's, if I would have just stayed at the airport and got on the flight to Anchorage, even after she said she wanted to stay with Kim, I wouldn't be here answering your questions and worrying about losing my job."

"You would have gotten over her that easy?"

McCarran pressed the heels of his hands against his eyes. "I don't know. Everything happened so sudden with her. I'd never been a head-over-heels kind of guy but then I was and … then it was over. Just like that."

"So you weren't just getting there in your relationship like you told me before, you were already in deep."

"Yeah, I guess."

"If you had a chance to see her again, if she had come outside before you left Kim's and you could take her somewhere and talk some sense into her, maybe rough her up a little. Anger, violence, another pattern, huh, Josh? "

"No, never with Shay. I only punched Kim's door when Shay sent that text that she was staying with Kim. But I left alone. I wandered around in Tent City, asking myself, what do I do now? I couldn't fight my way out of this one. I was so angry, I wasn't even looking where I was going. All of sudden I came up on those kids. When they started hassling me, I realized I still had Shay's stuff. Then all I wanted was to get rid of it, get out of there, go home, and get my mind right."

"That's quite a story. After Shalene dumps you, you're so angry you can't see straight, but instead of finding a way to confront her, you walk it off, go home and have a beer, and you're over her?"

"Not quite. There was still work. That's why I switched my shift. I didn't want to deal with her anymore. It made things easier."

"So you weren't thinking of making things easier for her by switching your shift like you told me before, you were making things easier for you."

"Both, I guess."

"You've also switched your story. Several times. Why should I believe this version?"

"I don't know, but I didn't kill her. That's the tru - -"

"Hold on," Active said as his phone chimed to signal an incoming e-mail. It was from Georgeanne at the medical examiner's office.

Two male workers in white aprons and hats replaced the empty bins at the steam table with new ones. Active caught the aromas of fish and something Mexican, maybe enchiladas.

McCarran drummed his fingers on the table and made a show of looking at his watch as Active read the email. "What is it?" He pushed back his chair. "I have to get back to work, so - -"

"Not yet, Josh. It seems the blade of that knife you had in Shalene's pack is consistent with the marks on her body."

Active held up his phone again and showed McCarran Georgeanne's email.

He glanced at it. "Consistent? That's not a definite thing, right? You can't - -"

"Definite enough." Active reached for his cuffs. "Stand

up and put your hands behind your back. Joshua McCarran, you're under arrest for the murder of Shalene Harvey."

GHOST LIGHT

CHAPTER EIGHTEEN

· September 2 ·

CHUKCHI

Active grabbed the edge of the wobbly *qanichaq* door of the old Atoyuk shack and wiggled it on its lone surviving hinge as he waited for Kavik. The rusted metal screeched.

Kavik came into view on the overgrown path from the beach and picked his way around the ropes that still cordoned off the site.

"What's up, Chief? I thought we were going to interview McCarran. What are we doing here?"

"The family attorney showed up this morning from Anchorage, and now Josh isn't talking. So, we're trying to come up with something else to connect the dots to him. " Active banged his palm against the door. "And this is the only dot we can be sure of."

"Chief?"

"We know this is where Shalene ended up. What we don't know is how she got here. McCarran was down here by his own admission, but there's no evidence she was with him."

"So we can't hold him?"

"Not for long. The best we can do is tie him to the blade found in the campfire and sweat him with that. But our twenty-four hours is about up, then we gotta cut him loose."

Active looked out toward the beach. Two clusters of a half a dozen or so people walked along the shore carrying bright yellow bags.

Kavik followed Active's gaze. "What's that about?"

"Beach Cleanup Day. Nita and some of her friends are participating. There's a big bonfire tonight to top it off."

"Oh, yeah," Kavik said. "It was on Kay-Chuck."

Active's eyes drifted to the campfire pit where they had dug up the knife blade. He pulled out his notebook, found the page he wanted, and ran a thumb down it.

"According to Shalene's text to Kim at 12:27 she was at the airport with McCarran. So why would she be down here?"

"Huh." Kavik looked up the beach toward the airport. "She and McCarran had a lot of time before the flight to Anchorage. They came here to pass the time, talk, have sex, whatever."

"She had her backpack along because it had her wallet, makeup, headphones, the stuff she planned to carry on the plane. But why the knife? Why wouldn't she put it in her checked luggage? She knew she couldn't get it through security."

Kavik frowned as if he wanted to say, why didn't I think of that? "Maybe she forgot?"

"Or ... well, hell. What if she was planning to use it on him?"

Kavik's eyes widened. "Why not just stay with Kim and let him go to Anchorage?"

"Because she would still have to deal with him at work," Active said. "This way he would be totally out of the picture. In any case, there's a confrontation, but she's the one who ends up dead. He hides the body, walks up the beach to where he ran into the kids, tosses her backpack with the murder weapon, and heads to the airport to leave it all behind."

"That's crazy. Why wouldn't he claim self-defense?"

"Because it is so crazy. Maybe too crazy for him to think anyone would believe him. Big guy, little girl. And he's got that juvenile record, and that violence at work."

Kavik frowned and thought it over. "Huh."

"He's had a night in jail to think things over. Maybe he'll talk if we dangle a reduced charge."

Kavik nodded. Then his eyes dropped to the empty spot on Active's belt. "Hey, where's your Glock?"

"Back at the office." Active stepped ahead of Kavik as though that was all there was to be said.

"But, what if - - "

"I'll use the AR-15 in the console."

"Chief Active, I'm curious as to why we're here." Josh McCarran's attorney, Alex Fortune, extracted a flannel cloth from his pocket, pulled off his gold-framed glasses, and polished the lenses. "Even your prosecutor, Ms. Procopio, agrees that knife is not enough to hold my client longer than twenty-four hours, and your twenty-four hours is about up. Maybe you've decided to release him early?"

Fortune and McCarran sat in the windowless interrogation room at the Public Safety Building across the table from Active and Kavik. Fortune was utterly hairless—not just bald, but devoid of mustache, beard, eyebrows or eyelashes. He wore a silver-gray three-piece suit and radiated money shine like a new Mercedes.

McCarran wore a blue inmate jumpsuit and looked like he needed a shower and a hairbrush after his night in Active's jail. A piece of lint, or maybe breakfast, was caught in his beard.

"We're here, Mr. Fortune," Active said as he opened his notebook, "because we want to give Mr. McCarran the opportunity to be more forthcoming about the death of Shalene Harvey."

Fortune's upper lip curled into a wry smile. "Mr. McCarran has told you all he knows. You don't have the evidence to support a murder charge. We both know that knife won't cut it." He smiled a little. "If you'll pardon my pun."

Active didn't smile back. "Mr. McCarran's story changes faster than our weather up here. What I want from him is the truth about how Shalene died."

McCarran leaned forward. His brows gathered in an angry frown. "I already told you I didn't kill - -"

Fortune gripped his client's forearm. "Josh, your job is to keep your mouth shut and let me do the talking."

McCarran crossed his arms and leaned back in his chair.

Active kept his eyes on McCarran. "Maybe you didn't mean to kill her. Is that how it was, Josh?"

McCarran remained silent.

"Was it her idea to go down to Tent City and hang out before your flight?"

McCarran's jaw tightened. "No. I didn't see her again after she went to Kim's. Not at Tent City, not anywhere."

Fortune gripped McCarran's arm again, harder this time. "Josh."

McCarran jerked his arm away.

Active ignored Fortune. "Maybe once she got to the airport, she wasn't so sure she had made the right decision. She suggested you take a walk, have a little talk. But she figured what she had to say might not go over so well. You've been known to get physical before. So, she took protection. Her knife."

"None of that happened. She never came back to the airport. I went to Tent City by myself."

"Or maybe she never planned to talk at all. She knew the town, she knew Tent City was an out-of-the way place where no one would be around to see the two of you. There was only one way to make sure she could go back to Kim and be safe from you coming after her."

"Coming after her? I told you I left on my own after I went up to Kim's and she wouldn't talk to me."

"That was silly of her, wasn't it, thinking a big, strong guy like you wasn't going to defend himself if a woman came at him with a knife?" Active paused. "Did she put those cuts on your knuckles?"

McCarran closed his arms across his chest, and closed his face as well.

"So. You struggled over the knife and somehow she got stabbed. You panicked, you cut her up, and you hid the body. Then you tried to cover it up by texting yourself from Shalene's phone that she was going back to Kim so we'd go after Kim if the body was ever found."

McCarran didn't speak.

"You can't get around hiding evidence, Josh, but manslaughter beats murder one." Active shot a glance at Fortune and continued. "This is your chance to get ahead of this. If it was an accident, or if it was self-defense, you need to tell me that now."

McCarran locked eyes with Active and stared for several seconds. "I beat my hands up on Kim's door," he said through gritted teeth. "I took the backpack off the four-wheeler in front of Kim's house. I didn't even know about the knife until those kids dumped it out. She never came to the airport. I went for a walk by myself. I didn't see her again. I didn't kill her."

Fortune stood up. "My client has nothing else to say, Chief Active. You don't have the evidence to support your charges and we're done here."

Fortune paused. His look said he was waiting to see if Active had any more ammunition.

Active nodded.

Fortune turned to McCarran. "Let's go, Josh."

McCarran rose with a bewildered expression, like, was it really this easy? He and Fortune walked out.

"Well," Kavik said after the door closed behind them. "We put out the bait, but the fish didn't bite. You really think it was self-defense?"

"Anything's possible. I figured it was worth a shot to try and push McCarran hard enough that he'd at least admit to Shalene being in Tent City with him. But maybe we're fishing in the wrong creek."

"Kim Tulimaq?"

Active took out his notebook and flipped through it to his first interview with her. "Here it is. She said she went to the airport at four-thirty or five the next morning to get the four-wheeler and was back at her place half an hour later. And she said she didn't go anywhere the rest of the day. Wanted some down time after the shock of Shalene leaving her, she said."

"Whereas McCarran says Shalene never came out to the

airport at all."

Active flipped through his notebook again. "Fortunately, Fred Sullivan's crush on Shalene might help us out."

"Sullivan? Oh, yeah."

"Right. Romeo Rick was knocking on Kim Tulimaq's door with a Chihuahua and a box of doughnuts that same morning around nine."

"Uh-huh," Kavik said. "I tracked down the taxi driver and she confirmed he was dropped off at that time and then picked up a few minutes later to go back to the airport."

"And Sullivan says Kim wasn't home. And her four-wheeler was nowhere to be seen."

"You think she was out taking care of business, like covering up a murder?"

"It's possible. Let's bring her in for an interview tomorrow," Active said. "And let's get Isaac Suyuk, that kid from the beach, in here, too."

"And his three pals?"

"We'll leave them alone, for now. Isaac seems like the one most worth questioning, as long as he keeps talking."

"Roger," Kavik said.

"Oh, and speaking of Sullivan," Active said. "He was where he said he was, and apparently had no more contact with Shalene, so we're done with him, right?"

"I'd say so, but …"

"But you'd like to bust him for those emails."

"Guy like that, Shalene probably wasn't the only one."

"But he's a key witness if we go to trial on this. How about we wait till we're done with him, then we rat him out to Molly at North Slope Environmental and let her decide?"

Kavik hooked a double thumbs-up. "Deal."

Active parked the Tahoe and walked toward the leaping flames of a big bonfire that was devouring a tower of cargo pallets and driftwood. As he got closer, he picked up the crowd noises--laughter, talk, the shrieks of children playing tag in the orange and yellow firelight.

He picked out the rhythmic thwack of an Inupiat dance drum and the cadence of an old chant from a group of elders on one side of the fire. Bruce Springsteen's "Born in the USA" rolled out of a boom box on the other side. From somewhere, the mournful strains of a harmonica drifted through the other music.

A quartet of kids in dark hoodies skewered hot dogs onto sticks to grill in the flames. A pair of teen-age break dancers, wearing sideways caps and baggy sweats, attracted a circle of clapping, shouting fans. A dozen or so of the older crowd lounged in lawn chairs or on Army blankets and blue tarps on the gravel beach.

Active recognized Isaac on the far perimeter of the crowd. His face was a wavy glow through the heated air coming off the fire. Active caught a whiff of marijuana in the wood smoke and spied Kinnuk Landon sitting on an Igloo ice chest with a joint in one hand and Buster in the other.

Active scanned the crowd for Nita and spotted her running his way, face alight.

"Dad!"

Three teen girls, the same size and shape as Nita, trotted behind her in puffy vests and jeans.

"Hey, kiddo," he said. She gave him an awkward side hug —because of the audience, he assumed—and he nodded to the friends. They smiled shyly. "How did the beach cleanup go?"

"We got second place." She held her phone out. "Look."

He swiped through the photos of Nita and her friends posing behind a huge stack of yellow trash bags, a bike with one wheel, a car tire, and a green suitcase with what looked like a stuffed toy hanging from the handle.

"Impressive." He handed the phone back. "How did the first-place team beat this?"

Nita rolled her eyes. "It was by weight. They didn't have as many bags, but they found a car battery and an airplane propeller."

"Are Mom and Charlie here?"

"Yep. They're on the other side of the fire, close in. We're going to roast weenies. See you, Dad." She gave a brief wave, and the four of them bolted away.

He threaded through the loose circle of people closer to the fire and sidestepped as a little girl careened past. His eyes followed her as she sped away, then he caught sight of Danny Kavik through the heat waves undulating above the fire.

And of the woman by his side.

Kavik with a woman? Kavik, whose private life had hitherto been a closed book? Yes, Kavik was definitely with a woman. His arm was around her waist.

"Hey, Danny." Active closed the few feet between them.

Kavik's companion wore a gray down vest over jeans, with a bubble-gum pink scarf draped loosely around her neck. Long dark hair cascaded past her shoulders from under a pale blue knit hat. She looked about five-five, half a foot shorter than Kavik.

"Chief." Kavik moved his arm from around the woman. "This is Lily Franklin."

"Nathan Active." He shook her gloved hand.

"Pleasure to meet you." She had a throaty voice and a smile that exposed perfect teeth, tilted up the corners of her brown eyes, and crinkled the sides of her snub nose.

Active guessed she was around forty, judging by the wings of gray at her temples and the laugh lines around her eyes. Forty, which would be something like ten years older than Kavik.

"Enjoying the gathering?" he asked her.

"Yes. I'd forgotten how the folks here seize on the slightest excuse to celebrate. I've been gone for almost thirty years."

"What brings you back?"

Lily paused for a few seconds. "It was time."

Active sensed there was some history here, history being brushed aside for now. "When did you two meet?"

She exchanged glances with Kavik.

"Seven, eight months ago," Kavik said.

"That long." Active winked at Danny and turned to Lily. "How have I not met you before?"

Kavik studied the ground with a look of embarrassment.

"My graduate work keeps me super busy," Lily said. "Danny had to drag me out here, even just for a couple of hours."

"Ah, you're Danny's anthropologist friend."

"Yes, technically still a student, but ..."

"Interesting. Your work, I mean."

"Oh, absolutely." She said it with another smile. "Yours too, from what I hear. Danny says you're working on a case that started with an elder looking for a *kikituq?*"

Active gazed beyond the couple into the fire. The case. It was never far away. An image of Tommie on the bridge passed like a shadow across his memory. He realized Lily was still talking.

"... like to interview her for my work."

"Good luck with that," Kavik said. "She lost her brain is how her husband puts it."

Active noticed Kavik's arm was around Lily's waist again. And his hand was brushing her hip. This was clearly more than friendship and anthropology.

"I was just about to meet up with Grace. You two want to join us?"

They exchanged glances again.

"We were about to look for Eddie, my son." Lily waved a hand at the assemblage. "He's around here somewhere."

"Oh, you have a little boy?"

"Not that little," Lily said. "He's almost a teen-ager. It takes a minor miracle these days to get him to go anywhere with his mom, instead of hunkering down in his room with his Play Station."

"Tell me about it. I have a teen-age daughter who just gave me three whole minutes of personal interaction. Find us later if you have time, okay?"

"Right," Kavik said. He nodded to Active, and the couple turned and walked toward the outside of the crowd, away from the fire.

Active found Grace seated on a quilt with her legs out and her upper body wrapped in her down throw against the chill from the water. Charlie's stocking-capped head peeked out where the throw draped across her chest. He appeared sound asleep.

"Hey, there's my snuggle buddy." She smiled up at Active.

He sat down, scooted against her and pecked her on the cheek.

"Looks like you've already got one." He kissed the top of Charlie's head and inhaled the scents of milk and baby. And of Grace's lavender perfume.

He put his arm around her and she pressed her cheek against his shoulder.

"I ran into Danny a minute ago."

"And that is making you grin like that why?"

"He was with his new girlfriend."

"Danny has a girlfriend. Our Danny."

Active raised his eyebrows. "*Ee.*"

"Well, good for him. What's she like?"

"Nice, smart lady, from what I could tell," he said. "Lily Franklin, grad student in anthropology. Seems like good people. Oh, and quite attractive."

"You go, Danny!"

"And apparently something of a cougar, as well. Gotta be forty if she's a day."

"Ooh, Danny's a boy toy now?"

"I don't judge."

"Older woman, younger man, that's the norm in some cultures, you know."

"What?"

"Oh, yeah. It has to do with when sexual desire peaks in each gender. It's later for us girls."

He bumped shoulders with her. "So you're saying I'm on my way down while you're on your way up?"

"Pretty much. But I'll probably keep you around, considering your other good qualities."

"*Yoi,* lucky me."

Grace leaned in and kissed him on the cheek. "Does this Lily have kids?"

"Kid. A boy, a little younger than Nita maybe."

"Great. If this gets serious, you and Danny can compare notes on raising teen-agers."

"I'm pretty sure we'll leave that to you ladyfolk."

"You would." Now she bumped his shoulder. "Of course you would. You saw Nita?"

"Yes. And the photos of the awesome second-place team."

"She was super excited, but she didn't think you'd make it to the bonfire. I'm happy you could get away from the case for a while."

Active squeezed her shoulder and gazed out at the light chop splashing onto the beach in the west wind. "It's like some missing piece is always tapping me on the shoulder and then I try to grab it and ... argh! It bounces away like when you drop a glove in a blizzard." He shook his head.

"You'll get there." She patted his thigh. "You always do."

Her touch was light, but it still triggered a spasm of pain in the injured thigh. He clenched his jaws, and masked his wince by pretending to adjust his legs.

"Yeah."

"That didn't sound very confident. Is something new bothering you?"

He watched the play of orange and yellow and flickers of blue in the flames. "No."

"No?"

"Okay, one thing is. Those photos Nita showed me of their trash haul."

"What would those photos have to do with the case?"

"They reminded me of ... I don't know, like when you see something and it makes you think of something else?"

"Like when I saw a lemon cake in the grocery store today and it reminded me I need to return the cake pan I borrowed from your mother."

"Close enough."

"So, what did you see?"

"There was this green suitcase."

"Oh, yeah," Grace said. "I took that picture. An old hard-shell suitcase, bright green at some point in its life, but not lately."

"I've seen a suitcase like that, but I can't remember where."

Charlie began to cry and root against Grace's chest.

"Snack time, I guess. Can you hold him for a sec while I get situated?"

Active cradled Charlie as Grace pulled up her sweater and pulled down the throw to cover the exposed breast. She took the baby and tucked him under. Within seconds he was latched on, sucking and grunting.

"You went to Anchorage a few days ago for that interview, right? Maybe you saw a suitcase like that in the airport? Check-in? Baggage claim?"

"Mm, maybe."

He watched Grace as she gazed down at a Charlie-shaped bulge in the throw, her quicksilver eyes aglow in the firelight.

Let it go, he told himself, the pain in his thigh, the case, Bachner, let it all go, at least for a while. This, right here, should be everything he needed.

So why wasn't it?

CHAPTER NINETEEN

· September 3 ·

CHUKCHI

"Ms. Tulimaq, thank you for coming in." Active said it with a polite smile as he and Kavik entered the Public Safety interrogation room. "You're just back from Deadhorse, I understand?"

Kim Tulimaq sat calmly on a folding chair and sipped from a bottle of water. "Special three-day training. But, happy to help if you need some more information about Josh McCarran."

"I appreciate your willingness to cooperate, but that's not really what I want to talk about."

"You arrested him for killing Shay, right?"

"I see the Chukchi grapevine is working with its usual efficiency." Active shook his head. "Mr. McCarran has been released. I expect he's already back on the Slope."

Tulimaq's shoulders tensed, but otherwise she didn't react.

Active took out his notebook and pen and made a show of flipping through the pages to let Tulimaq stew.

She adjusted her legs, folded her hands on the table, returned them to her lap. "Well?"

Active looked at his notes for a few more seconds.

"I just need to clarify some of the statements you made in our previous interview." He lifted his gaze from his notes and watched her eyes. "You stated that you picked up your four-wheeler at the airport the day after Shalene left, at four-thirty a.m. Is that correct?"

"Give or take a few minutes, yeah." She folded her hands on the table again.

"And you were back home at ... "

"Around five, I guess."

"Give or take a few minutes?"

"Yeah, five-ish."

"Did you go anywhere after that?"

"Like I told you, no. I got home about five, and I stayed home the rest of the day."

Active nodded and scribbled on his pad. "What did you do at home?"

"Mostly stayed in bed." Tulimaq's lower lip trembled. "It was a tough day."

"So your four-wheeler would have been in front of your house the whole day?"

She cocked her head and looked a little cornered. "Yeah. I didn't go anywhere."

"Well, that's odd." He paused and looked at Kavik, who nodded.

"Really odd," Kavik said.

"Your boss, Fred Sullivan, dropped by your place later that morning," Active said. "And he says nobody was home."

"Fred? What the hell was he doing in Chukchi, and why would he come to my house?"

"He came bearing doughnuts."

"He brought doughnuts? That's just creepy."

"He was looking for Shalene. Did she ever talk about Sullivan as anything more than a supervisor?"

"Are you kidding? He was way too old for her."

"Sometimes a girl will have daddy issues. Like if Shalene had trouble with her father when she was a kid, you know ... "

Tulimaq screwed up her face and hissed, "No, I don't know. And that's disgusting."

"Sullivan knocked several times but no one answered."

"It could have been a little later when I got back with the four-wheeler, closer to six or maybe seven. I forgot before. I went by my *aana's* to check on her, maybe talk to her about Shay. *Aanas* are always good for that, ah?"

"And how was she?"

"Fine. She was asleep in front of the TV. I cleaned her kitchen, put away the dishes, and waited for her to wake up, but she didn't. So, I let her rest and came home."

"And you think you got back at seven?"

"Yeah, something like that."

"Well, Sullivan was there around nine and he didn't see any four-wheeler."

"Oh, yeah, I parked it behind the house so I could unhitch the trailer back there."

"Actually, it turns out your boss is kind of a snoop. He went looking around out back, peeked in the windows, that kind of thing. And guess what? No four-wheeler there either."

"Well, he ... he must be wrong. How you gonna believe a perv like that anyway? I left it out back. If he didn't see it, maybe he had other things on his mind."

"Maybe you did, too." Active wrote again on his pad.

"You forgot about visiting your *aana* and you forgot where you parked your four-wheeler."

Tulimaq stared at her hands in silence.

"Where were you around nine a.m.?"

Tulimaq unfolded her hands, put them back in her lap, scooted her chair closer to the table, then scooted it back, and took another swallow of water.

"Nine? When Fred came by? I never heard anyone knock. I took one of those pills to help me sleep. Like I said, it was a tough day."

"What was the name of the medication?"

"It was that over-the-counter stuff, Z something. I don't take it much. It gives me crazy dreams."

Active had a brief flash of his own midnight replays of the shootout on the bridge, then yanked himself back to the waking world. "Did you have crazy dreams that day?"

"Yes." Her eyes filled and she brushed away tears. "I dreamed Shay and I were together at Serpentine Hot Springs. Down by Shishmaref? We went there on vacation in March. Those were happy times."

Happy times. The words hit Active with a jolt. "Right. Like with the photos in your bedroom."

Tulimaq smiled uncomfortably. "I should have put them away, but …"

"Did you and Shalene take a lot of trips together?"

"A couple, I guess."

"That photo of the two of you with your luggage, you look like you're off to somewhere exciting."

She smiled and looked down at the table like she was lost in the memory.

"Shalene must have been the flashy one, right?"

Tulimaq looked up and frowned. "What? Why?"

"That bright green suitcase with the little purple bear hanging from the handle. In the photo?"

"Oh, yeah, that was totally Shay."

"Did she take that suitcase when she went off with Josh McCarran?"

"Yes, I saw her pack it and load it on the four-wheeler."

"Do you have any idea how it ended up on the beach?"

It was a bluff, but how would she know?

She didn't.

"You found a suitcase like that on the beach?" She shrugged. "A lot of people have green suitcases."

"Not with a purple Teddy bear on the handle." He watched for Kim's reaction. Maybe she flinched, just slightly. Maybe not. Mainly, she just looked thoughtful.

"But once we get the blood inside tested and matched to her DNA …"

"But, that's not foolproof, right? If the suitcase was on the beach all this time or maybe even in the ocean - - you can't get DNA from something like that, right?"

"You'd be surprised what the crime lab can do, so we'll see. But you didn't answer my question."

"What question was that again?"

"If she was at the airport with Josh like you said, how did her suitcase end up on the beach?"

Tulimaq closed her eyes for a moment with the same thoughtful expression. She opened them but didn't speak.

"You know what I think?" Active said. "I think Shalene never made it to the airport. She never left your house alive, but her suitcase did because you had to get rid of it."

"She WAS at the airport with him! I showed you her text where she said that. And she left here with that green suitcase."

"Why wouldn't she check it at the airport?"

"I don't know. Wait, Josh texted her that the plane was delayed, remember? Probably they went for a ride to Tent City while they were waiting and that's when he killed her, before she ever had a chance to check her baggage. Then he ditched her stuff where he thought no one would find it."

"So Josh abandoned the suitcase on the beach? Or threw it in the sea and it washed up on the beach?"

"Who knows what he did, but that makes the most sense."

"Except we know Josh was on the plane to Anchorage at 4:45 p.m. This was the middle of May, when the sun doesn't set till after midnight. Do you really think a strange white man with a bushy beard would take a chance on being seen in daylight on the beach getting rid of a bright green suitcase if he killed somebody? See, what makes more sense to me is, if Josh was the killer, he'd check that suitcase before getting on the plane. Then he'd dispose of it in Anchorage, and no one would be the wiser."

"Killers do stupid things, right, they're crazy? That's how they get caught."

He had to admit she had a point. If Josh had killed Shalene, it was unpremeditated, something done in the heat of the moment. He had been violent in the past, but he wasn't an experienced killer. He had never gone that far. And if he was in a time crunch to make his flight and escape Chukchi for Anchorage, he could have decided to cross his fingers and take a chance on the suitcase.

Whereas Kim would have had plenty of time to plan how to get rid of the evidence, and she seemed to have an answer for every question he threw at her.

Was he dealing with a sloppy killer or a meticulous one?

He closed his notebook and met Tulimaq's eyes. "Sometimes killers get caught because they try too hard to outsmart the cops."

Tulimaq held his gaze without blinking.

He thanked her for her cooperation and asked Kavik to see her out. Moments later, he was back with Isaac Suyuk.

Active pulled Kavik aside and spoke low so Isaac wouldn't hear. "I'm not sure how he'll do with two cops in the room."

"I can watch through the one-way mirror," Kavik said.

"Sounds good. And pull our prints of the employee ID photos of Josh and Shalene from their files. I'll signal when I want you to bring them in."

"Right."

"And call Public Works and find out where they put the trash they collected on the beach yesterday."

"What are we looking for?"

"A neon green suitcase with a purple Teddy bear on the handle."

GHOST LIGHT

CHAPTER TWENTY

· September 3 ·

CHUKCHI

Isaac Suyuk was hunched over the table when Active took his seat. The boy looked like he was trying to take up as little space as possible.

Active guessed, as in their previous talk, that Isaac would be more inclined to open up if his shriveled self-esteem could be bolstered a little.

"Hey, buddy, you want a soda before we get started?" Active asked.

Isaac blinked hard, nodded, and worked his mouth into a response. "Sp-sp-sp-Sprite, p-p-p-please," he sputtered.

Active turned to Kavik, unseen behind the one-way mirror, and jerked his head toward the door.

When Kavik came with the drink a couple of minutes later, Isaac grabbed it as if somebody might yank it back unless he took immediate possession.

"Are you about ready to leave for UAF?" Active asked as the door closed behind Kavik.

"Yes, s-s-sir," Isaac said. "I leave tomorrow."

"Where you gonna be staying out there?"

"My sister and her kids. They got a tr-trailer."

"It's nice you've got family to stay with, all right."

Isaac half-smiled and raised his eyebrows, then slurped from the drink.

"I bet you'll miss your friends, though, right?"

"Yes. Are you t-t-talking to them, t-t-too?"

Active took out his pad and pen. "Actually, you're the one we're counting on to help us with our investigation." Active guessed that, other than their last talk, Isaac had never had a chance to act as spokesman for his crew.

"The m-m-murder investigation."

"Yes. We can count on you, right?"

Isaac blinked hard again. "I th-th-think so. But what if I can't answer your questions?"

"Just be honest and do the best you can, okay? If you don't know the answer, you tell me. It's okay."

Isaac nodded and his shoulders relaxed a fraction of an inch.

"You and your friends were hanging out at a campfire on the beach soon after high school graduation in May, correct?"

"Yes. May fifteenth. I looked it up after you ta-talked to me before," Isaac said.

His stutter was easing up, Active noticed. He took it as another sign Isaac was relaxing a little. And that he would almost certainly not try to lie.

"How long did you and the boys hang out at the beach?"

"Three hours, maybe. Until all the beer was gone and the fire was going down."

"You saw the white guy with the beard that day. Did you see him earlier that same day up in Tent City?"

"We never went up there that time. That place is deserted when no one's around for fish camp yet, so we just stay on the beach."

"You're sure none of you went up there that day? You or the boys didn't go up there on May fifteenth, maybe check out some of the old camps, have a smoke?"

"Nah. We go stay there with Big's auntie in the summer sometimes. She'll put up her wall tent and cook lotta fish, mm, *aarigaa!* But not in May, no fish yet. She's never in Tent City till the fish come in."

"When you saw the white guy walking toward you at the campfire, what direction was he coming from?"

"From down the beach. We're close to the north end and he's walking toward us from the south."

"Could he have been up in Tent City?"

"He could have, all right. I didn't see him come down the bank to the beach, but he could have."

"Now, I want you to think hard about this, Isaac. Did the white guy say where he had been or if he was with anyone?"

"No. He just say he's gotta go to the airport."

"He didn't mention anyone else?"

"He got that pack from somebody, so it must've been that g-g-girl, ah?"

"He mentioned a girl?"

"I don't kn-kn-know."

Isaac was tensing up again, but Active sensed it wasn't because he was lying, just that he felt under pressure.

"No problem, that's exactly what you should say if you don't know. Just think about it a little, picture that day when he came up to the campfire. What did he say?"

Isaac looked down at the table, and closed his eyes. "When Kenny grabbed the pack, that *naluaqmiu* said, 'That's hers' like he got it from a girl."

"Okay, Isaac, I want to be clear here. When I talked with

you before, you said Kenny grabbed the pack and the man didn't say anything. Are you sure he spoke?"

Isaac ran a hand through his hair, producing a cowlick at the back of his head. "Kenny scared him, all right, so all he said was, 'That's hers,' but Kenny, he took the pack anyway."

"Did he say the girl's name?"

Isaac pulled at his jaw. "No. He never said a name."

"Did he say he was meeting anyone at the airport?"

"Probably that girl, because he had her pack. I bet she was mad she didn't have it, ah?" Isaac snorted a brief laugh.

"Did he say he was meeting the girl at the airport, or did you just figure out that was what he must be doing?"

Isaac ran his hand through his hair again and frowned in concentration.

Active gave him a few seconds. "I need you to be absolutely positive when you describe what you heard, Isaac. Did the white man say he was meeting the girl at the airport?"

"No, I as-s-sumed. He never said anything like that."

Active paused to scrawl some notes. "Was this bearded man carrying anything else besides the girl's pack and his own backpack?"

"No, I'm p-p-positive."

"He wasn't carrying a suitcase?"

"A suitcase? No. I would've noticed a suitcase, ah?"

"Yeah, I guess you would. You're very observant."

"My dad always say, 'Isaac, maybe you don't talk so good, but you sure notice everything.'"

"You talk just fine, Isaac."

That brought a smile, one of the few Active had seen from Isaac.

"I just have one more question. Did you see a young

woman around that area earlier in the day, a Native girl, pretty? Maybe the Nome girl on the driver's license from the pack?"

"No, nobody else, just me and the guys, and that *naluaqmiu.*"

"Okay, Isaac, that just about wraps it up, but there's just one more thing."

Active waved in the direction of the one-way mirror. Kavik came in with two photos, set them face down in front of Active, and stepped back to lean against the wall.

Isaac stretched his neck to see. "Wha-what are those?" he asked.

Active turned over the picture of Josh McCarran and pushed it toward Isaac. "Have you ever seen this man?"

Isaac's eyes widened. "That's him." He tapped the photo with an index finger. "That's the *naluaqmiu* with the bloody hands."

"You're sure? Absolutely sure?"

Isaac bent over the photo. "He wasn't smiling like that, but it's him, all right."

"Okay." Active turned the second photo over and slid it next to McCarran's. "Do you recognize her?"

Isaac's face was blank for a few seconds. He picked up the photo and studied it, then put it down and smiled. "Yes, I saw her before."

"Again, are you sure?"

"Yes, I saw her before, all right."

"Where did you see her?"

"At E-Z Market."

"E-Z Market?"

"Yeah, in the newspaper. She's that girl got killed. That one they found dead in Tent City, worked on the Slope."

"Do you remember her from anywhere else?"

"No. I just heard about her on Kay-Chuck. Then I saw her picture in the paper. That's too bad what happened." He tapped the photo of McCarran again. "Is this the guy killed her?"

"We're not sure yet, but you've really helped us try to figure it out." Active closed his notebook. "If you remember anything else, let me know." He slid his card across the table.

Isaac looked disappointed that the interview was over. He was relaxed, legs splayed, arms stretched across the table. He drained the soda, pushed back from the table, and stood up. When he walked out of the room he stood a little straighter, Active thought.

Kavik came in and dropped into the chair vacated by Isaac. "Do you think he's telling the truth?"

"That's how it felt to me. You?"

"The same."

"But we're no closer to connecting the dots," Active said. "Seems like we're just picking up more loose ends."

"Like Kim Tulimaq's sudden memory of checking on her *aana* on her way back from the airport."

"But if she was asleep, how can she verify anything?"

"You know, some of those old *aanas* sleep with one eye open."

"Good point, I'll pay her a visit- -"

He checked his watch. It was coming up on 6 p.m., a little late in the day to start a serious conversation with an elder.

"- - first thing in the morning," he finished.

Kavik nodded.

"And what did you find out from Public Works?"

"The trash is piled up on the beach. It's supposed to go to the landfill tomorrow afternoon."

"All right, let's hit it right after I talk to Millie. Let's put somebody on it tonight, so nobody messes with it, oaky?"

"You got it."

GHOST LIGHT

CHAPTER TWENTY-ONE

· September 4 ·

CHUKCHI

"You need some tea, ah?" Millie Tulimaq said in her high, crackly voice. It was a statement, not a question.

Active settled himself at the old woman's yellow kitchen table in the little cabin a block from the Catholic church.

Two hind-quarters of caribou lay on a couple of big sheets of cardboard on the floor. The meat was partly carved into steaks and strips in a pile surmounted by an *ulu*. Minnie, it appeared, followed the old Inupiat custom of conducting the important business of the house on the floor—cutting meat and fish, sewing furs, perhaps even playing the rambunctious multi-handed variant of solitaire known as snerts.

Millie shuffled to the stove, lifted a singing kettle, and poured him a cup of tea.

"Thank you, Ms. Tulimaq."

She reminded him of the healer Nelda Qivits. So much so that he expected the bitter tang of sourdock as he lifted the tea to his lips. But, no, it was much milder. A raspberry taste that was only a little bitter.

Millie set out a dented aluminum camp saucer stacked

with Sailor Boy Pilot Bread, along with a knife and a jar of peanut butter. He hadn't had breakfast yet, and his mouth watered at the thought of Sailor Boy. He spread peanut butter on one of the pancake-sized crackers, took a big bite, and let his eyes close in bliss. There was nothing better than pilot bread with peanut butter. Nothing.

"You like your Eskimo food, ah, *naluaqmiiyaaq?*" Millie said with a grin.

"Of course if it's Sailor Boy."

"You gonna be a real Eskimo yet, you stay around here."

Active grinned at her teasing. He'd been in Chukchi long enough to marry and have a child. But the old-timers still ribbed him without mercy about being a *naluaqmiiyaaq*—almost white—because of his upbringing in Anchorage by white adoptive parents.

"Pretty soon, ah?" he said.

Millie chuckled and lowered herself into a chair. Her dark eyes gleamed from a brown face, now somber, framed by silver braids. "You come to talk about my Kimmy, ah? She's in some kinda trouble?"

"I just have a few questions."

She blinked, and her expression softened in patient anticipation, tinctured perhaps with caution.

"You live by yourself?"

The old woman nodded. "Long time now, almost thirty years, since my husband pass."

"Your granddaughter says you're a strong woman."

"I try stay busy, go to bingo, sing with my church ladies, do my beading, cook for the elders at the Senior Center."

Active took a bite of Sailor Boy and peanut butter. "And watch some TV?"

A broad smile crinkled her face. "I like that 'Bachelorette' show, all right. I never miss that one, them little girls are so pretty. I watch the news sometimes, but too much politics, same thing all the time, I fall asleep."

"Does Kim come by to check on you?"

"Ah, she don't come so much no more. Don't want to listen to her *aana*, I guess." She shook her head.

"Do you remember when was the last time she came by?"

She shook her head again. "Some time before breakup, I think. Seem like she was on her snowgo."

"Was she much trouble when she was a kid?"

"Not all the time. She keep to herself a lot, never talk much. I worry she'll keep everything inside after her mom die, then her dad and stepmom get kill."

"Killed? I thought they died in a fire."

"*Ee*, the house burn all right. But they're already dead when it happen and then someone start the fire, that's what they say. *Arii*, on their first day married, too."

"Was anybody ever arrested?"

Millie folded her hands on the table. "No, they never catch 'em."

"Did Kim get hurt?"

"They find her outside in the shed, hiding from the people did that. She almost die from cold by then. My poor Kimmy, so skinny and all close up inside when she come stay with me. I try take care of her best I can. Even now she's a woman she still can't talk about what happened, just go up to her camp, hunt, fish, pick berries. Then when she come back she'll say, 'I'm okay, *aana*. Don't worry.' But I know she has pain. I always pray for her, all right."

Active eyed the crucifix above the sink. He had passed another in the main room when he came in.

Millie massaged the fingers of one hand with the other.

"Is she in trouble?"

"I'm just following up as part of an investigation. We don't know that she did anything."

Millie's face went bland and unreadable, as happened with elders when they didn't quite believe you but were too polite to say it. She folded her hands again on the table. He thanked her and eased out, feeling the dark eyes on his back as he closed the door.

Back in the Tahoe, he started for the beach and called his old Trooper boss, Pat Carnaby.

"Need more advice, Nathan?"

"No, just a little information if you can dig it up."

"Same case?"

"Yep." Active heard a munching sound through the phone and a slurp. He must have caught Carnaby in the middle of lunch. If he knew Carnaby, it was a double bacon cheeseburger and a Coke, not Diet. Exercise program or not, some habits evidently could not be broken.

Carnaby smacked and swallowed. "You know me. If I can't find it, it can't be found. Whattaya got?"

"House fire in Nuliakuk maybe fifteen years ago. Two fatalities, a male and a female. Possible double homicide or murder-suicide, and possibly arson. Apparently went cold and never got solved."

"That would have been a little before my time, but...yeah, I remember hearing about it. That kind of thing doesn't happen much around here."

"There was a child that survived. Teen-age girl, found outside with severe hypothermia."

"What does a fifteen-year-old cold case have to do with a murder that happened a few months ago?"

"The survivor's a person of interest in the Tent City

murder. Kim Tulimaq."

"Huh," Carnaby said. "I'll get on it. I think I remember the guy that had the case. He's retired now but if I have it right, he's down in Klawock."

"All help greatly appreciated."

"Give me a couple of days maybe. Sure you don't need any more advice on that other thing?"

"I'm sure."

"Because you're handling it."

"Absolutely. And you're handling that cheeseburger and Coke."

"Gimme a break. It's a veggie burger. And green tea."

"Of course it is. Thanks again."

At the beach, Active found Kavik beside a ten-foot mound of bulging yellow trash bags a few yards from the ashes of the previous night's bonfire. A hundred bags, plus or minus, Active calculated.

A red-and-gray garbage truck was parked close by. Some of the bags had already been loaded. The driver, a sixtyish Inupiaq wearing a red cap and a frown, jumped down from the truck and walked toward Active and Kavik.

"Unbelievable," Kavik said.

"That our citizens found this much litter on our beach?" Active asked with a grin.

"No, that we have to go through it."

Another police Tahoe pulled up with Alan Long and an officer named Jenkins in the front seat.

The Public Works driver came up, and he didn't look pleased. "If yesterday wasn't the Labor Day holiday this would all be gone already," he said. "We gotta get this junk loaded and dumped at the landfill by four or I gotta ask for overtime again. *Arii,* the boss don't like that."

Active checked the ID tag on his zipper pull. "Mr. Oktollik, is it?"

The driver raised his eyebrows and they exchanged a single-pump handshake. He eased around Active to put the west wind off the bay at his back, then hunched his shoulders and pulled down a Native Pride ball cap as the wind stiffened a little more.

"We'll get it done as fast as we can," Active said. He turned up the collar of his jacket and huddled into it. "You might be able to help us. We're looking for a suitcase about yea big." Active stretched out his hands about three feet apart.

"A green hard-shell with a little purple Teddy bear tied on the handle. You seen anything like that?"

"Naw. Trash is trash, ah? It might be with the stuff that was too big to bag. It's in those piles over there."

Oktollik pointed to two other mounds a few yards off. Active saw several car tires and the propeller blade Nita had mentioned.

"Good. We'll start with those."

He waved the other officers over. They pulled on leather work gloves and started tugging one pile apart while Active and Kavik worked on the other.

Kavik grunted and flung aside a dented and rusted oven door.

"So you and Lily ..." Active said.

"What?"

Active yanked at a tire. It slid down the pile and hit the gravel with a thud. "You're broadening your horizons, huh?"

"Meaning?"

"They say a seasoned woman can teach a young man a thing or two."

"I already know a thing or two, thank you very much."

"Is that right?"

Active tugged at a twin-size box spring. Kavik grabbed the opposite side and they extracted it from the pile.

"It's more like we're learning from each other," Kavik went on. "There's a mutual respect, not just an attraction." He clapped his hands to knock off the accumulated dust and dirt. "She's an amazing woman."

Active was taken aback for a moment. He had expected some standard male banter about the new girlfriend, but this tone, this was new for Kavik.

"Wow. Sounds serious."

"Could be. Don't know yet."

"I kind of get the impression you're keeping it on the down low?"

"Not me. Her. She's nervous about the age difference. You know how women hate being judged, especially by other women."

"Tell me about it. But she does seem like a great lady. And she was a local girl at one time?" Active tossed aside a broken snowgo ski.

"Yeah. Her mom took her and her sisters Outside when she was little. She grew up in Oregon and stayed there."

"And she decided to come back because ..."

"Her mom died last year. Her sisters had married and moved away. The way she explained it, she wanted to reconnect with her culture, make peace with her past."

"Peace with her past. What's that about?"

"Not sure yet," Kavik said. "I figure, give her the space and time, and she'll tell me when she thinks I'm ready to hear it."

"Sounds right to me." Active spotted a rounded green

corner of something hard and shiny behind a three-legged chair.

"Bingo!" he said.

Kavik muscled the suitcase out onto the beach gravel. Its side was dented, but Active was sure it was the suitcase from the photos on Kim Tulimaq's wall. A misshapen blob of plush hung from the handle. He made out the ears and snout of a stuffed Teddy bear. The legs and belly were squashed, and the color had faded to a pale lavender after months of immersion in Chukchi Bay or exposure on the beach.

Active dismissed Long and his partner, then laid the suitcase on the ground. Kavik went back to Active's Tahoe for a camera.

Active inspected the suitcase inch by inch while Kavik shot photos. It still had its wheels and the telescoping handle was still intact, although it couldn't be pulled out all the way. Active scraped green slime from the case's side with his thumbnail, producing a small square of the original neon green.

The zipper had partially separated, and it was easy to pry the case open the rest of the way. The inside held a few handfuls of sand and slimy seaweed. The bottom and the empty fabric pockets were soiled with black and rust-colored streaks. Dirt, grease, blood, sea salt, who knew?

"No ID," Active told Kavik as he slipped the suitcase into a trash bag and carried it to the Tahoe. "But the color and size match the one Shalene had. And there's that Teddy bear on the handle."

"Maybe Kalani can figure it out."

Active slid in behind the wheel. "Let's hope."

"It could have been on the beach long before Shalene

was killed," Kavik said as he climbed into the passenger side.

"Or dumped in the bay long after," Active said.

GHOST LIGHT

CHAPTER TWENTY-TWO

·September 5 ·

CHUKCHI

Active rooted through his desk drawer for an old bottle of Rolaids he remembered seeing there at some point in the past. The Aortic Dragon egg rolls he had wolfed down for lunch weren't giving up without a fight.

Kavik walked in and headed straight for the coffee pot. "Have you heard from the Anchorage lab yet?" he asked as he poured.

"I was just gonna call." Active found the Rolaids in the farthest corner of the drawer and tossed four of the tablets into his mouth. "Bleah!" he said as the chalk dissolved on his tongue.

He dropped into his chair and punched the lab's speed-dial button on his desk phone.

"Chief Active, what can I do for you?" Kalani's words rumbled out of the earpiece like a double bass. The tech at the Anchorage crime lab had the deepest voice Active had ever encountered in a human being.

He put the phone on speaker so that Kavik could hear the conversation, and to spare his own ear.

"Kalani, long time no talk."

"Just got back from the islands. I had to go for my *puna wahine*, my grandmother. All the family came for her ninetieth birthday."

"One thing Alaska and Hawaii have in common, we celebrate our elders."

"May it always be so. But you didn't call to talk *ohana*, family, yeah?"

"No, not this time. I was hoping you might have something for me on that green suitcase."

"I was going to call at the end of the day, but I don't expect there'll be anything more. What I can tell you is that it was in salt water for a long time, weeks at least, maybe months. I can't determine whether it was submerged for all of that time or only part of it."

"Did you find anything that might identify the owner or in whose possession it might have been?"

"Sorry, can't help you much there. Tons of stray fingerprint smudges, probably very recent. Those will take some time to sort out."

"Probably from the kids who found it during our beach cleanup," Active said. "I wouldn't worry about anything that looks too recent. What about the Teddy bear?"

"Combination of synthetic fibers like your average stuffed animal, mostly made in China, sold everywhere, nothing unique The color was dark purple at one time judging from the roots of the fibers."

"What about the stains on the inside?"

"We found traces of blood, but we can't pull any DNA from it or even be sure it's human. The sample is too degraded. Other than that, some gravel, sandy soil and some kind of small-engine lubricant."

"Thanks, if you find anything else - -"

Active's cell rang, and Nita's number came up. He was about to hang up to catch the call before it went to voicemail when Kalani spoke again.

"Chief, I almost forgot. We got something else for you."

"Yeah?"

"You sent me those two rings?"

"Yeah, from near where the body was. A plain silver one and the other one with a scroll design."

"Those are the ones. The descriptions say they belonged to the same person?"

"They both came off the victim, as far as we know. Is that a problem?"

"Not a problem, exactly, but a discrepancy at least. It would be odd if they belonged to the same individual. The plain silver one is a size eight, the other one is a six, two sizes smaller."

"Is that a big difference? I don't know much about rings, other than never to take off my wedding band."

Kalani's chuckle rumbled out into the room.

"Pretty big difference," he said. "If the size eight fits you, then the size six is gonna be real tight. You might not even be able to get it on. And if the size six fits you, then the size eight is gonna be real loose. Its gonna try to slide off the minute you put it on."

"Huh." Active punched up Nita's voicemail on his cell. "That is odd. If you turn up anything else on the suitcase, let us know, okay?"

The office phone rang the moment he hung up, and Nita's number came up on the display. He dismissed the voicemail on his cell and scooped the receiver out of its cradle.

"Hey, kiddo," he said. "How's my favorite daughter?"

"*Arii*, that is such a Dad joke. I'm your only daughter."

"Wouldn't matter how many I had, you'd still be my favorite."

"But what if you and Mom have another baby and it's a girl?"

"Then she'll be my favorite daughter, too. Just like you."

"You always do this."

"All part of the Dad job. So what's up?"

"Kinnuk Landon is here."

"At the house?"

"*Ee*," she said. "He's on the deck with his cat."

"He brought Buster? What's he doing?"

"Looking out over the lagoon and drinking a Coke."

"Kinnuk Landon? A Coke? Not a Budweiser?"

"Uh-huh," Nita said.

"What does he want?"

"He said you and him should talk now. I said to go to your office, but he said he'll only talk here and he'll wait on the deck. I don't think he wants anybody to see him go into Public Safety. I gave the cat some of Lucky's chow. It looked so skinny."

"Did he say anything else?"

"He said he's ready to voice out that Annie girl and you'll know what that means."

"I do. Tell him I'll be right there," Active said.

When Active arrived a few minutes later, Landon was still on the deck, with a bottle of Coke between his forearms as he leaned on the wooden railing. He was looking out over the lagoon, where the west wind had ruffled the water up into little whitecaps.

Beside Landon's left elbow on the railing, Buster was at work on a bowl of Lucky's Alpo.

Landon turned and watched as Active approached. The cat looked up, blinked once, and went back to the Alpo.

It took Active a moment to figure out what was different about Landon today. It wasn't just the soda, he decided. It was that Landon was clear-eyed and his hair was tied back in a neat ponytail and perhaps even clean. Plus, his clothes looked less wrinkled than usual and also cleaner.

"Hey, buddy," Active said. "How you doing?"

"Same, I guess."

"I don't know. You look pretty good." Active pointed at the Coke. "No Budweiser or weed?"

"Not today, I guess."

"You talked to Nelda, ah?"

"*Ee.*"

"Uh-huh."

"She make me feel...I dunno. Different."

"Better, maybe?"

"*Ee,* she really help me. Early days ago, maybe she'd be an *angatkuq,* the good kind that always help people."

"Ah-hah, I think she would have been." Active leaned on the railing beside Landon. A half mile south of the house, the levee that supported Chukchi's main runway stretched across the lagoon. A single-engine Cessna lifted off and swung north along Cemetery Bluff behind the lagoon. Active turned to Landon.

"You feel like you could voice out Annie now?"

Landon took a long drink of Coke, then pulled Buster into the crook of his left arm. "*Ee.*"

Active laid his phone on the railing and tapped the Recorder icon. "I need to record this, okay?"

"*Ee.*"

"It was what you say," Landon began. "Annie never kill

herself. Everybody at the party's in the kitchen or the living room, drinking beer, watching basketball on Roger's widescreen, talking and hollering, when Annie come out and yell at them to quiet down, she can't get the baby to sleep."

"Roger tell Annie, 'Bitch, it's a fucking party,' then he drag her into the bedroom," Landon went on. "I hear them screaming at each other and then there's a slap like he's punching her, then she screams even more and the baby start screaming, too."

"Nobody went to check on them?"

"No, they're all used to it, I guess, but that baby screaming, that really scare me. I run open the door, Roger and Annie are fighting over a gun. And then Roger, he, he ..."

"Take a minute, buddy," Active said. "Just go ahead when you're ready."

Landon looked at Buster, dipped a finger into the Alpo, and came up with a dab of brown goo. He held it out and the cat licked it with a delicate pink tongue.

"So Roger and Annie were fighting over a gun?" Active prompted.

Landon drew in a deep breath. "*Ee.* Then Roger put that gun in Annie's chest and it go off and she fall to the floor. That's when he look up and see me."

"Nobody else came in when they heard the shot?"

"No, not right away. Roger say real quick, 'You saw her, she did it herself, man, you got that? Or you're next.' Then he throw the gun on Annie's chest and run out yelling, 'Annie shot herself!'"

"What did you do?"

"I grab the baby out of the crib and put him in my coat and run outside and call the hospital for an ambulance to

Roger's house. Then I get on my bike and take the baby to his *aana*. Then I go home."

"And you never told anybody what really happened?" Active asked.

"Not till you," Landon said. "That Roger, he's, he's...he scare me."

"Don't worry about him, I'm going to lock him up in my jail." Active pointed at the phone on the railing, still recording. "This is what I needed."

He took Landon through it once more and clarified a few details, then put out his hand and they exchanged a long shake. At the end of it, Active pulled Landon into and embrace and clapped him on the back.

"You're a good man, Kinnuk. A really good man."

GHOST LIGHT

CHAPTER TWENTY-THREE

· *September 5* ·

CHUKCHI

The photos Lucy had printed off of Kim Tulimaq's Facebook page covered nearly every inch of Active's desk. For more than an hour, he had been staring at them, shuffling, and staring again. Something about Kalani's call wouldn't let him stop.

But what was he looking for? Nothing new jumped out at him. The same smiling faces, two people in love, a young couple going places, sharing time, sharing space, having fun. Nothing in them said, "One of you will soon be stabbed through the heart, cut up like a caribou, and left to rot in a falling-down shack."

He pushed the photos aside. Better to tie up the loose ends on a case where that was actually possible.

He called Theresa Procopio, let her know that Kinnuk had finally come through on their cold case, and requested an arrest warrant for Roger Aiken for the murder of Annie Ramoth.

Then he gave Carnaby a ring and asked him to pick up the suspect because the Public Safety force was too busy at the moment.

"Sure, we can go over and arrest him," Carnaby said. "But seriously. Kinnuk actually came through? Our Kinnuk Landon? How the hell did you pull that off?"

"I told him he was a good man. Repeatedly."

A knock sounded at the door as Active rang off. Kavik poked his head in.

"Yeah, Danny, whatta we got?"

Kavik dropped into a chair. "Nothing new, I guess, unless Kalani pulls off a miracle with our suitcase."

"Or comes up with something new on those rings, but how likely is ..."

Active stared at the center photo in the pile on his desk. Kim and Shalene smiled back, hands out, side by side, showing the matching scrollwork rings.

"What?" Kavik said.

"The rings."

"What about 'em?"

"Dammit!" Active snatched the photo and held it out to Kavik. "Look at this! Their fingers are different sizes. Shalene's are much bigger."

Kavik peered, nodded, and frowned. "And?"

"And we recovered two rings at the body site. The plain silver ring, the larger one, is the one that McCarran gave Shalene. The other one, the one with the scrollwork, is two sizes smaller, according to Kalani. It's also one of the rings in this photo."

"Right," Kavik said. "Kim and Shalene exchanged rings. They're the same."

"Except they're not. They're not even close to the same size. So the one from the body site can't be Shalene's. It's much too small to fit on her finger."

"And since they had matching rings, if it's not Shalene's -

_"

"Then it has to be Kim's," Active said.

"And the only way Kim's ring could be at the body site is
_ _"

"- - is if she hid the body there!"

Kim Tulimaq's turquoise house was quiet when Active and Kavik pulled up in the Tahoe ten minutes later. Afternoon sunlight glinted off the front window. The curtains were drawn. No smoke spiraled from the stovepipe, no four-wheeler was parked in front.

Active stepped into the *qanichaq* and took stock. The gun and stacked plastic buckets he'd seen on his first visit were gone.

He gave the inner door a three-rap civilian knock, then waited out a ten count. Nothing. He escalated to the seven fast hammer blows of his cop knock. Still nothing.

"Kim Tulimaq!" he shouted in his command voice. "Chief Active, Chukchi Public Safety. We have a warrant for your arrest for the murder of Shalene Harvey."

More nothing.

He tried the door. It was locked.

Kavik came into the *qanichaq* from a quick check of the rear of the house. "No four-wheeler, but the kitchen door's unlocked."

They circled to the back and Active eased into the kitchen, Kavik a pace behind him.

"Kim Tulimaq," he said again. "It's Chief Active." The dead, still air was silent.

The counters were devoid of even a single crumb, the stove scrubbed free of grease splatters, the stainless-steel sink polished and shiny. Striped dish towels hung in a neat row from the handle of the oven door. Active detected a faint odor of bleach.

Computer printouts of photos were scattered across the kitchen table. Active recognized them as the pictures from the mirror in the extra bedroom. He motioned for Kavik to check the rest of the house and studied the photo in the center of the table. Kim and Shalene posed with big grins and blue-purple juice running down their chins. Between them they held a Mason jar of blueberries. The handle of a wooden spoon stuck out of it.

"All clear," Kavik called from the living room.

"Berry picking and hunting," Active said. "That's what her *aana* said she does to get her head together. At her camp on the Katonak. I think there was a photo of it on her Facebook. And I'm guessing Millie gave Kim a call after I talked to her and tipped her off, probably without meaning to. We need to get up there."

"Cowboy Decker?"

"He flies hunters and fishermen out into the country all the time. I'll bet he'll know where that camp is if he sees that photo."

"I'll call Lucy and have her send it to his phone."

"Good idea." Active pulled out his own phone and showed Kavik the pilot's number. Kavik put in the call to Lucy as Active tapped Cowboy's contact.

The call went to voicemail. "I need you, buddy," he told the recording. "We need to get up to the Katonak as soon as possible. Call me."

"Photo's on its way," Kavik said. "We heading to Lienhofer's now?"

"First let's check the bay for Kim's four-wheeler."

A half-hour later, they found Cowboy in the Lienhofer break room, scrawling in his pilot's logbook, brow furrowed in concentration.

He looked up with a surprised expression when Active cleared his throat.

"Nathan? What are you doing here?"

"You haven't checked your phone lately, I'm assuming?"

The pilot patted his pockets, then turned up his palms. "Crap, I must have left it in the john. Hang on a minute."

He disappeared into the men's room and came out studying the photo of Tulimaq's camp on the screen of his phone. "What's up?"

Active explained the situation and they piled into his Tahoe and headed for the Chukchi airport's float pond.

"You're sure she's up there?" Cowboy said a few minutes later as they walked out to where his Cessna 185 was nosed up to the shore of the float pond. Cowboy always put his Bush workhorse on floats for the summer, then switched back to wheels or skis for the winter.

"Pretty sure," Active said. "We found her four-wheeler parked by the bay at what looked like a boat tie-down. So we're thinking she might have gone up to her camp. You know the place, right?"

"Absolutely."

The pilot took a last deep pull on his Marlboro and flicked it into the water. He climbed onto the left float and walked along the side of the plane to a little door near the tail. He opened it, fished out hip boots, and leaned his rump on a wing strut to pull them on.

"I recognized the place as soon as I saw the photo," he said as he stepped down off the float. "I flew her and her friend out there to hunt last fall. I can put you down on a little lake about a half mile back on the tundra."

The pilot jumped into the water and motioned Active and

Kavik to help him push the plane off the shore. Once the Cessna was afloat, Active and Kavik splash-stepped out to the nose of the right float, climbed up, and boarded.

Cowboy swung the plane around to point away from the beach, then climbed into the pilot's seat as Active's cell erupted and Carnaby's number came up.

"Hey, Pat, whattaya got?"

"No 'how are you today?'" Carnaby asked.

"Sorry, we're kinda rockin' and rollin' here."

"Gotcha. So, yeah, that cold case in Nuliakuk? The man and woman both had their throats cut while they were passed out drunk in bed, judging from the liquor bottles scattered around the house and in the bedroom. Then whoever did it apparently poured stove oil everywhere and set the place on fire. The evidence was pretty skimpy since the house was basically reduced to ashes and they originally thought the fire was accidental. It wasn't till they did the autopsies that they realized they had a double murder on their hands and started a real investigation."

"They have any suspects?" Active asked.

"Well, there was this belligerent neighbor that the guy got into it with over some kind of fight between their dogs, and the woman had a sketchy ex-boyfriend. But both of 'em had alibis and they never found the murder weapon. No one else lived in the house except your very own Kim Tulimaq."

"Was she a suspect? Did they test her clothing or hands for stove oil or - -?"

"She was barely fourteen, Nathan," Carnaby said. "I know this job makes you hard, but - - anyway, her clothes and hair were singed. She was terrified, half naked, and near dead from the cold when they found her. She had cuts on her fingers and palms, fairly deep ones."

"Defensive wounds."

"To all appearances. So they never looked at her as anything but a victim."

"What did she say when she was interviewed?"

"Nothing, apparently. Too traumatized to talk. She got farmed out to her grandmother."

The propeller jerked once, twice, and a third time, then the engine coughed to life as Active buckled himself into the copilot seat. "Gotta go," he told Carnaby. "Thanks, I owe you one."

"Way more than one," Carnaby said. "But I won't hold my breath I ever get paid."

The Cessna roared down the float pond, lifted off, rolled right, and climbed out over the choppy gray waters of Chukchi Bay.

A few miles ahead, the Katonak River fanned out in a vein-work of meandering channels as it finished its journey down from the Brooks Range and emptied into Chukchi Bay.

Far upstream, white-crested ridges incandesced in the afternoon sun slanting under the overcast. The weather for the past few days had mostly been mild, more summer than fall. But soon enough, Active knew, the snow on the ridges would spread down the valleys, and one day the first blizzard of the season would howl in from the east and bury Chukchi in long-tailed white drifts.

"There it is," Cowboy said a few minutes later through Active's headset.

Active looked out over the left float at a tin-roofed cabin of turquoise plywood that squatted in the woods a few yards back from the bank of the Katonak. An Alaska flag flapped above the door, and a silver aluminum skiff with a big white outboard on the back was pulled up to the water's edge below the cabin.

A thread of smoke curled out of a stovepipe in a corner of the roof before it disappeared into the grayness of the sky. An unidentifiable heap of gear lay near a spent campfire, but there was no sign of Kim Tulimaq.

"I'd put you down in the river there if I could," Cowboy said. "But it's real shallow and rocky along through here, so it'll have to be the lake I was telling you about. Call me on the sat phone when you're ready to come out."

He dipped the wing, circled back, and dropped the Cessna onto a small lake, barely more than a pond, a half mile from the cabin. The floats threw up rainbows of spray as the sun drifted toward the horizon.

Cowboy nosed the Cessna up to the shore and shut down. Active and Kavik climbed out, walked to the noses of the floats, jumped down, shoved the plane back into the water and started through the scrub spruce toward the turquoise cabin.

Behind them, the Cessna coughed back to life and roared off the lake as Cowboy headed back to Chukchi. An Arctic fox, still in summer gray, peered from an alder thicket, sniffed the air twice with what struck Active as disdain, and trotted away.

In another ten minutes, Active and Kavik were easing up to Tulimaq's camp. Kavik's hand was on his holstered Glock, Active had slipped the AR-15 off his shoulder and brought it around to waist level, muzzle pointed down forty-five degrees. If Tulimaq hadn't heard Cowboy's arrival, she would almost certainly have heard his takeoff, and it was a given that she was armed.

CHAPTER TWENTY-FOUR

· September 5 ·

TULIMAQ CAMP, KATONAK RIVER

"Kim Tulimaq!" Active called from beside the trunk of a big spruce ten feet from the cabin door. "Chief Active and Officer Kavik, Chukchi Public Safety! Come out with your hands in the air! We have a warrant for your arrest for the murder of Shalene Harvey."

Silent seconds ticked past. Active peered around the spruce as he waited.

Tulimaq appeared in the cabin doorway wearing a red vest, jeans, and a baseball cap.

And a bolt-action rifle strapped across her back. The thumb of one hand was hooked through the sling, meaning the weapon could be whipped into action in a second or two. The other hand rested on the hilt of a belt knife at her waist.

Kavik drew his Glock. Active brought up the AR-15 and peered down the barrel at Tulimaq.

"Drop that weapon and put your hands up!" he shouted.

Tulimaq inched forward until she was outside the door and raised her hands to shoulder level, the rife still slung across her back. Active's palm was damp on the grip of the AR-15. His heart raced as he waited for her arms to continue upward.

Then she was running, bolting to the right of the cabin and away along the river bank, the rifle bouncing against her back.

Active motioned for Kavik to circle behind the cabin and started after Tulimaq as she hurtled through the trees. He had cut the distance between them to about twenty yards when she stumbled and fell to her knees.

He stepped behind another big spruce as she whirled and pulled the gun over her head in one swift motion and held it across her chest.

"Drop that weapon or I will shoot you!" Active brought the AR up, steadied it against the spruce trunk, and trained it on her chest. "I will shoot you."

She collapsed to a sitting position, cross-legged, the rifle across her lap and pointing away from Active.

"Kim! Put down that weapon!" he shouted. "Nobody has to get hurt here."

"I want to be alone," she shouted, her words almost lost in the wind sighing through the spruce boughs. "I want you to leave!"

From the corner of his eye, Active caught Kavik easing through the trees toward Tulimaq from behind.

"You know we can't do that." Active dropped to one knee—closer to Tulimaq's eye level—and lowered the barrel of the AR a few degrees. "Look, I talked to your *aana* and I know you've been hurt before when you were abandoned by somebody you loved."

"I needed him!" she wailed. "After my mom died, I needed somebody to take care of me. I was just a kid! But he married that slut and then it was all about her."

"Is that why you did it?"

"They found me outside. I was so cold. They said both of them died in the fire."

"But you knew better, right?" A fine, cold mist began to sift down from the gray sky. "You were just a kid, that was amazing what you did. You slashed their throats while they were passed out, then you set the house on fire. You must have barely made it out without burning up yourself. You were scared to death when they found you, but not of the fire. You were scared of getting caught. And those cuts on your hands. Did that happen when you were killing them or did you do it yourself so you'd look like a victim, too?"

"I don't want to talk about that."

"And the knife. What did you do with it? I mean, you were fourteen years old."

"I said I don't want to talk about it!"

"That's okay, we don't have to. Let's talk about Shalene."

"I loved her!"

The gun rocked on Tulimaq's thighs. Active cut a fast glance at Kavik. He was only a few yards off now, slipping from tree to tree.

"I know, I know. If only Josh McCarran hadn't come along …"

"He was bad for her," Tulimaq said. "But she couldn't see it!"

A bolt of pain stabbed through Active's injured thigh and suddenly he was on the bridge again, the man jumping out of the truck and bracing a rifle on the hinge of the open door and starting to shoot, the jolt in Active's hip as the bullet hit.

Cold sweat beaded on his forehead and the AR-15 jerked up and aimed itself at Tulimaq's heart under the red vest. His finger tightened on the trigger. He waited for her to make a move, any move.

Long, agonizing moments ticked past. Finally he forced himself to talk again.

"Was that what you argued about, how Josh was bad for her?"

"We argued, but we made up. She said she would always love me."

"But?"

"But she was leaving with Josh anyway. We were in the kitchen. I was cutting sheefish. She came up behind me and put the ring I gave her on the counter next to my knife."

Her voice was lower and sadder now. Active strained to hear.

"I asked her for one last hug and I smelled her hair and I ..." A minute of silence passed. "Those arms around me...her body so warm...her breath on my neck."

Gulping, wrenching sobs mingled with the moist air. Two Canada geese passed over, their honks like cries of mourning.

"The knife was in my hand and sliding into her before I even knew what I was doing. She looked in my eyes and I saw she was surprised about dying and she said 'Oh, Kim, all our moments.' Then she was gone."

Tulimaq was silent under the drizzle and the sighing spruces, immaterial as a ghost in the drizzle and fading light.

"I couldn't let her leave. You understand? I couldn't."

She looked down at her left hand and twisted the band on her ring finger.

"I do understand, Kim, and I am so sorry for your trouble. And now, I need you to understand something. We have to take you back to Chukchi."

She shifted at the shoulders. Active trained the AR on her chest again, but she didn't touch the rifle in her lap.

"It's going to be a cold, wet night, Kim. You don't want

to be out here by yourself."

"*Arii,* I miss her so much. I was better when I was with her." She stood, lifted the rifle, still pointed away from Active, and levered a round into the chamber.

Active jumped to his feet, the AR sights still on her. "Kim! Drop that weapon! Do not make me shoot you!"

"Go ahead!" And then she was rising and spinning and swinging the rifle toward him and he was firing and the stock of the AR was thumping against his shoulder and she was going down, screaming and pitching the rifle away and clutching her elbow, and Danny was storming out of the brush from Active's right and planting his knee on her back and cuffing her good arm to her belt.

Active crossed the mossy forest floor to the takedown, cleared Tulimaq's rifle, and tossed it a few yards farther into the woods, then secured his AR as the panic welled up out of his stomach and tried to take over. Sweat ran down his cheeks and trickled out of his armpits and his legs went wobbly as he leaned against a spruce to fight it off, thankful that Kavik was too busy over Tulimaq to notice.

In a few moments, it started to seep away and Active drew in a deep, slow breath. He let it out with a soft whoosh.

Kavik passed Active the Buck knife from Tulimaq's belt and pulled his first-aid kit from the vest he wore under his jacket.

Tulimaq screamed as Kavik eased her onto her back and cut the sleeve off the injured arm to expose a shattered, bloody elbow. Active spotted a spearpoint of bone protruding through the skin.

"Lucky the bullet missed the brachial artery," Kavik said as he worked. "Otherwise we'd be talking tourniquet here and you never want that. Especially in the field."

"*Arii*, it hur-r-r-r-rts," Tulimaq moaned. Her eyes drifted shut and her head lolled back.

"Kim!" Kavik shook her but got no response. "Kim, stay with me here!"

He slapped her.

Her eyes opened and she said *"Arii."* The eyes closed again.

Kavik checked her pulse. "Shit, she's going into shock." He pulled a plastic pillbox from the first-aid kit.

He shook her and slapped her again. Finally her head came up a little and her eyes opened.

Kavik shoved a tablet into her mouth. "Swallow it!" he said. "Swallow, dammit!"

Her jaw tightened and her throat muscles worked as the pill went down. Kavik lowered her back to the forest floor.

"She gonna be all right?" Active asked.

"I think so. The oxycodone should take care of the shock."

He studied the patient, then took her pulse again.

"Yeah, better," he said. "But we need to get her out of here. If a bone shard in that elbow cuts the brachial, it's gonna be life and death."

"Can she walk back to the lake?"

"I think so," Kavik said. "If we help her and take it slow. If not, I guess we can rig a stretcher somehow.."

"I'll get Cowboy on the way." Active stabbed the Buck into the trunk of a spruce, pulled out his sat phone and punched in the pilot's number as Kavik put a sling on the injured arm.

Kavik stood up and studied the knife in the spruce for a moment. "Huh. Instead of your bullet passing through her elbow and tearing her up inside, look what stopped it."

"My bullet? How do we know it wasn't yours?"

"I never got a shot off," Kavik said. "When she jumped up and spun around, it put that tree between us." He pointed at the spruce with Tulimaq's knife sticking out of it. "By the time I got clear, she was down and screaming with the busted elbow and her rifle was eight feet away."

Active leaned in, sat phone to his ear, and examined the knife's handle. There was a crater where the resin had been shot away down to the steel, and the steel itself bore a dent the size of a nickel.

"That's where your bullet hit after it went through the elbow," Kavik said.

"A knife saved her life?"

"High probability."

"Jesus," Active said as Cowboy answered the sat phone. "What a day."

It was warm in the cabin, shirt-sleeves warm, from a barrel stove that popped and crackled in the corner. One wall bore a framed photo of Kim and Shalene showing off their rings, the same shot that was on Facebook.

Tulimaq sat on a metal cot, huddled under a sleeping bag draped around her shoulders. Her good arm was cuffed to the cot frame, her bad one immobilized in the sling. She was more alert now. Not all the way alert, but neither was she almost out like she'd been before Kavik's oxycodone had kicked in. She studied them from under hooded brows.

Kavik found a jar of tea bags, pumped up the white-gas canister on a camp stove on the counter and put water on to heat.

Active gave Tulimaq the Miranda warning.

She dropped her gaze to the ring on her bad hand peeking out of the sling. "*Arii*, why would I care about that now? You should have killed me."

"I almost did. That knife saved you." He pointed to the Buck on the table beside his AR-15.

She studied the damage to the handle, then the ghost of a bitter smile crossed her lips. "*Yoi*, so lucky."

She shivered and pulled the sleeping bag tight around her. "When is that plane gonna be here?"

Active checked his watch. "Another half-hour maybe. We'll start for the lake when he buzzes the cabin."

Kavik poured hot tea into a mug, then held it to Tulimaq's mouth so she could sip without the use of her hands.

"That must have been quite a day you spent in the house with Shalene's body," Active said. "What was that li- -"

"Cutting her up, that was pretty hard, all right," Tulimaq said in a low, flat voice. "But it was the only way I could get her out of there."

The rage and grief they had seen outside was gone. Maybe it was the oxycodone, but Active didn't think so. It seemed more like she was describing a movie that played in her head.

"She didn't bleed hardly at all when I stabbed her, so I guess my knife must have gone straight into her heart. I laid her down on the floor with the hole in her side pointing up, undressed her, put some ice bags around her, and waited for the blood to cool."

Active suppressed a shudder. "What did you do all that time you were waiting?"

"Finished cutting up the sheefish, wrapped it, put it in the freezer. Then Josh was pounding on the door and that was scary, but he was easier to get rid of than I thought he would be. I wouldn't have given up on Shay that easy, but I guess you know that."

She gave a short, sharp laugh that was half sob, half bark, then studied the ring again.

"By nighttime, her body was real cold. I made a couple of test cuts, she didn't bleed, so I knew it was time. I spread out a blue tarp and put a sleeping bag on it and put her on top of that and went to work. She didn't hardly bleed at all."

She shifted on the cot, adjusted the injured arm, winced, and grunted. "Can I have another pill?"

Kavik checked his watch. "Not yet." He walked over and held the mug while she took another couple of sips of tea.

"How long did it take to cut her up?" Active asked.

"Not that long," Tulimaq said. "All you have to do is cut the ligaments and then the joints come apart real easy, doesn't matter if it's a caribou or a bear or an *inuk*." She chuckled. "One time when I forgot my Buck I cut up a caribou with a pocket knife."

She uncrossed and recrossed her ankles, and winced again as the movement jostled her injured arm. Blood from her wound had seeped through and made a red-brown patch on the sling.

"The head was the hardest. I couldn't stand her looking at me. I had to stick duct tape over her eyes."

"Why hide the body in Tent City?" Active asked.

"I wasn't sure where at first, then I thought about that shack with the old Eskimo ice cellar. We used to go there and smoke weed in high school. It was just a matter of packing her up. I had trash bags and totes, and I used one of her suitcases, the green one. I loaded everything on my little trailer early the next morning while it was still dark, hooked up my four-wheeler, and off I went."

"What about those texts from Shalene's phone?" Kavik asked. "We thought maybe it was Josh for a while."

"Pretty smart, ah? I thought that would throw you guys off if anybody ever found her." She smiled to herself. "I took her phone, my knife, everything out on the ice with my four-wheeler, weighed it down with rocks and old snowgo parts, and threw it in an open lead. Then it was gone forever."

"Except the suitcase," Active said. "The green suitcase. Somehow the sea threw it back."

"So, what? You couldn't be sure who took it out there."

"No, but we could be sure about the ring Shalene gave you," Active said. "We found it at the body site. That's when we knew you had to be the one that put her there."

Tulimaq look at them, eyes narrowed, chewing her lower lip in thought.

"So that was it," she said. "If only she wasn't wearing that cheap ring Josh gave her when I was cutting her up. It was like she was mocking me, lying there naked with nothing on but that ring. I snatched it off and got the ring I gave her from the counter and put it back on her. But then when I got down to Tent City, I thought, well, what if she's found with my ring still on her finger? Then it would look like she stayed with me instead of going off with Josh. I tried to get it off again, but, it was stuck. I guess her finger was starting to bloat up by then. So I cut it off to get the ring loose and I slipped it in my pocket. And, since I had Josh's ring with me, I tossed it in the cellar by her body so it would look like he did it."

"But then you lost your own ring, the one Shalene gave you." Active asked.

She grimaced. "*Arii*, so dumb. I didn't even know it was

missing until I got home. I thought it must have come off while I was cutting her up, 'cause things got kinda slippery. I looked and looked, but it wasn't anywhere in the house, or anywhere around the body when it got dark that night and I went back to Tent City. I was kinda *kinnuk* for a while there, all right, trying to figure out where it was. All I could do was hope it slipped off while I was out on the ice or if I lost it in Tent City, it would stay lost. Then I took Shay's ring out of my pocket and put it on. It was loose, but it looked exactly like mine and I liked having that little part of her on my finger. Who would ever know?"

"A really smart Hawaiian guy in Anchorage."

Tulimaq looked mystified, but Active didn't explain. She was silent for a long time. Then, with a wistful look, she talked again.

"I always tickled her to wake her up in the morning because she would snort when she laughed too hard. I teased her about it and called her my little walrus and she would say, '*Arii*, you always do that.'"

She paused and looked from Active to Kavik to Active again. "Those little things, that's what love is, ah?"

"Except you killed her," Active said. "Did you ever think, if you were right about Josh being wrong for her, she might have figured that out and come back to you?"

Tulimaq's face went cold. "She didn't get to leave me."

GHOST LIGHT

CHAPTER TWENTY-FIVE

September 7

CHUKCHI

Active pulled the Tahoe up to the Leokuk house on Caribou Way.

Oscar let him in, pumped his arm once, and motioned him to a seat in the low-ceilinged, overheated living room. Tommie sat nearby in a plush, blue armchair, hands folded in her lap. She wore the same sweet smile and vacant stare as the day she had delivered her first "souvenir" to his office—the partial jawbone of Shalene Harvey.

It seemed like a long time ago, but in reality less than a month had passed.

He pulled the evidence baggie from his pocket, took out the carving, and let it rest on his palm. A flat whale head with fierce teeth, filed to points, a body with the muscular back legs and tail of a dog.

"Mrs. Leokuk, is this what you were looking for?"

Tommie's blank stare vanished and her dark eyes sparkled. A child smiled out as she plucked the carving from his palm.

"*Kikituq!*" She thrust the little monster at Active. "Owr-r-r-r-rr!"

Then she slipped it into the pouch of her *atiqluk*.

"Her grandfather was an old-time *angatkuq*," Oscar said. "I guess he gave it to her when she was just little. Thank you for returning it."

"My pleasure. Without Tommie and her souvenirs, we wouldn't have caught a killer. I'm the one who's grateful."

Back in the Tahoe, Active called Grace and caught her on the way home from work.

"Sweetie, I might be a little late for dinner. I have to take care of something first."

"Not that case again," Grace said. "I thought it was done."

"It is. Kim Tulimaq was arraigned this morning and charged with second-degree murder. This shouldn't take long, just a quick thank-you to someone who helped us out with a different case."

He steered the SUV west toward the corner of Caribou and Third, then north to Nelda Qivits's little cabin.

The hunched, white-haired elder answered his knock and peered up at him. She studied his face for a long moment. The waning sunlight flashed off her huge-lensed glasses and almost blinded him.

She beckoned him in with a gnarled hand. "You come for sourdock tea, ah?"

"No, I just came to say *quyaanna* for talking to Kinnuk Landon. After he talked to you, he came and told me how Annie Ramoth really died, and now we arrested Roger Aiken for it."

She beamed. "*Aarigaa,* it's good when I can help."

She studied his face again. "You should come in, all right."

"No," he started to say, "I need to get home for dinner."

But what came out was *"Ee"* and he found himself

following her bony old form into the kitchen. He took a wooden chair that creaked under his weight.

She filled the dented kettle, set it on the back burner, and unwrapped a twisted root from a piece of cloth.

He fidgeted with the doily in the center of the table as she steeped the tea. Suddenly, he felt her gaze on him. It was warm and soothing like sunlight bouncing off a snow bank in the spring.

"You still talking to that Anchorage guy?"

"Not as much now, no. I've been handling it myself, mostly."

She set a yellow mug of the nasty-smelling tea in front of him and lowered herself into the chair across the table and sipped from her own mug.

"Well, look to me like you need somebody really going to help you. Somebody can take out the poison like you can't do by yourself, ah?"

He stared down at his tea, felt a spasm in his lower lip. He bit down on it to hold everything in.

Nelda nudged the tea closer to him. "Maybe don't talk now. Just sit for a while, ah?"

The cat-shaped clock on the far wall ticked off the seconds. It sounded like a hammer in the small, silent room.

Active raised the mug to his lips. He sipped the tea. He set the mug down again. The tears came all at once as he began.

"I knew a man named Bachner," he said. "He was like me."

The End

ACKNOWLEDGMENTS

The authors wish to express their deepest gratitude to the following people, whose support and assistance made this book possible:

Mark Borchardt, a Bush pilot in the finest sense of the word, for ride-alongs over the Alaskan Arctic.

Norm Hughes and the other men and women of the Kotzebue Police Department, for much useful information on how policing works in the Alaska Bush, and for ride-alongs on patrol on spring evenings in the Arctic.

Jim Evak of Kotzebue, for his help with the Inupiaq language and many other particulars of life in the Arctic.

And friends, family members, and fellow writers too numerous to name who reviewed the manuscript along the way and recommended countless improvements.